A Latte Mayhem
Joss Miller Mysteries, Book 2

Tyora Moody

Tymm Publishing LLC

A Latte Mayhem
Joss Miller Mysteries, Book 2

Copyright © 2024 by Tyora Moody

All rights reserved. No part of this book may be reproduced or transmitted in any form or by any means without written permission of the author.

A Latte Mayhem is a work of fiction. Names, characters, places and incidents either are products of the author's imagination or are used fictitiously. Any resemblance to actual persons, living or dead, events, or locales is entirely coincidental.

Published by
Tymm Publishing LLC
www.tymmpublishing.com

Paperback ISBN: 978-1-961437-20-3
Ebook ISBN: 978-1-961437-19-7

Cover Design: TywebbinCreations.com
Editing: Felicia Murrell

Chapter 1
Stirring Mayhem

Tuesday, June 11, 10:05 a.m.

There were only a few times in my life when I'd felt my body floating, even though I was standing still. I could hear the murmur of conversations around me. Even the mixed scents of freshly brewed coffee and sweet cinnamon rolls didn't break my focus.

Really, it was only a few seconds. But the longer I laid eyes on the man in front of me, the warmer my body felt.

"Okay, I would normally say you two need to get a room, but Ms. Joss Miller here is supposed to be working. Detective Baez, don't you have some case to solve?"

I tore my eyes away from the handsome detective, my cheeks warm from embarrassment, and looked at my boss. "Um, I was giving Detective Baez his order." I snuck a glance at him. "He's such a faithful customer."

Fay crossed her arms, she eyed me and then Detective Baez. "Really, Joss." She shook her head before heading to the back of Sugar Creek Café.

Detective Andre Baez came into the café every morning like clockwork. I told him he was a café resident now. We had several patrons who visited daily. While he loved our special blend of coffee, he was also my boyfriend.

Boyfriend.

I often wanted to pinch myself. We'd been dating for almost eight months. And I was very much in love.

The way Andre gave me his full attention, I felt pretty sure he was smitten with me too.

He grinned. "Sorry. I didn't mean to get you in trouble."

I waved my hand. "It's fine. Fay's been in a mood the past few days. I don't know if you heard, but the Davis family down the street is closing their boutique. They're on the other side of the Book Nook. So there will be two empty storefronts on this block."

Andre let out a slow whistle. "Really? That's got to be tough. I thought everyone was united in not selling."

I shrugged. "That's what I thought, but apparently Rick Nelson worked his magic. Plus, Mrs. Davis is up in age and she's been trying to get one of her children to take over the shop for years. I think she's tired. Money looked good toward her retirement."

This all started late last fall when the owner of the craft store next door, the Crafty Corner, was killed. There was quite a bit of fallout from Maggie Nelson's death, including her younger brother, Rick Nelson, inheriting the property. Rick decided to shut down the craft shop, and for the past nine months, he's been fixated on a campaign that would bring in developers. His primary goal – to build a luxury hotel.

It would only be a matter of time before Rick Nelson started hounding Fay about selling the café again. He sent a letter late last year, which both Fay and her fellow business owner, Albertine Lancaster of the Book Nook verbally protested at a city council meeting. Fay was pretty popular on social media and brought her grievances to her followers, who flooded Nelson with online posts opposing his antics.

However Rick tried to come at Fay, he would have to tread carefully.

I knew how much Fay loved this place. The café had been like home to me, and Fay had been really good to me. Not only as a mentor, but also like a big sister. When I struggled a few years ago to find my way, she gave me a chance. I'd always loved coffee, but being a barista hadn't really crossed my mind. Now I was

Fay's right hand woman, the assistant manager of Sugar Creek Café.

"Tell Fay it will be okay. The café has quite the fanbase, and Rick Nelson doesn't." Andre's cell phone beeped.

I watched as he removed the phone that was hooked to his belt. His eyebrows creased as he read the message. Then he reached for his coffee cup and looked at me. "I need to go."

"Do you want a refill?" I hoped he would hint at what had worried his handsome face.

He shook his head. "Thanks, I'm good. I'll see you tonight."

"Okay." My mood dropped a bit as the familiar door chimes rang and he headed out. I wondered where he was going and if it was a new case. I looked around Sugar Creek Café taking in the cozy atmosphere. The thought of losing all this to some soulless redevelopment project was even more depressing.

I walked in the back to check on Fay. I found her at her desk, staring at the laptop. "Are you okay?"

Fay sighed. "Yeah. I'm sorry. I'm glad you two are still going strong."

"Me too." I hadn't had the best track record with dating and had taken long extended men fasts in between.

"Have you talked to Mrs. Davis? Any chance she might change her mind."

"Unfortunately, no." Fay frowned. "She said Rick offered her more money than she could ever imagine, but I felt like there was something else she wasn't telling me."

"Like what? Do you think he tried to intimidate her?"

Fay sighed. "I wouldn't put it past Rick Nelson. You know more than most that the whole family is a bunch of bullies."

Yes, I knew that well. The Nelsons and I had crossed paths too many times for me to care.

Still, I asked a question that I already knew the answer to. "Do you think Rick Nelson is going to pressure you?"

Fay smirked. "I have no doubts that he will try. He's probably going to leave me for last. I just hope other business owners don't cave to him. I don't want us to be left standing alone."

I heard the chimes of the café door, a customer had arrived or left. "Hang in there. Let me go out and take care of this customer."

My gaze swept the customer at the counter, and my heart broke a little. Claude McKnight. The café was practically a gallery of sorts featuring all kinds of artwork by this very talented artist. One of my favorite pieces was one I commissioned him to do for me.

A large portrait of my grandfather August Manning, a charismatic young man from this community whose life was cut short fifty years ago, was seen by the many people that graced our doors.

As I approached the counter, I put on a smile to hide my concern. Claude was a handsome man, but he always looked like a starving artist. He spent most of his mornings sleeping, rising late in the afternoon and painting until the early hours of the next morning. So it was unusual to see him in the café at this time of day. And today, dirty blonde hair unkempt and dark circles under his eyes, he appeared more disheveled than usual.

"Hey, Claude," I greeted him. "What can I get you?"

He gave me a small smile. "I'll take an espresso and one of those banana nut muffins."

"Sure thing." After he swiped his card, I said, "I'll bring it out to you."

"Great." He turned to look around the café. "I'm going to talk to Eleanor."

Eleanor Olsen was one of our regular café residents and a local mystery author. Claude's deceased father and Eleanor had been friends all their lives. I'd often wondered if the never married Eleanor had unrequited feelings for Claude's dad. She talked about him fondly and looked after Claude like he was her own son.

A LATTE MAYHEM

I added Claude's order to a tray and walked over to Eleanor's table. "How's it going, you two?"

Eleanor smiled. "It's been a good morning, especially now being around two of my favorite people."

I grinned. "I appreciate you, Eleanor."

I placed the tray in front of Claude. "Is everything okay?"

He took a sip of the espresso and sat for a few seconds, almost like he needed the liquid to boost his energy before responding. "It's been hard these past few days."

His eyes darted around nervously as if he was afraid someone might overhear. "I know I can share this with you two," he admitted. "You know about my friend Rebecca Montgomery, right?"

I nodded. "Yes, she went missing almost three years ago now."

Eleanor asked, "Has there been any breaks in her case?"

Claude crossed his arms and then uncrossed them, placing his hands on the table. "The anniversary of her disappearance was Saturday. Her sister came by the studio last night. She seemed to want to talk, but then she started asking me all kinds of questions. The same ones she asked me last year and the year before last. I finally asked her to leave."

"Oh no, I'm so sorry, Claude. It's crazy how Rebecca disappeared, and all this time no one knows what happened. I know that must eat away at her sister."

Claude placed his hands over his eyes as if he wanted to shut out the world. Then he blew out a breath. "I know Olivia and Becca weren't all that close, but they were it. Their mother died years ago. I don't know why, but Olivia suspected me from the beginning. The police suspected me too. Even though I don't know anything, I can never really get out from underneath people's suspicions."

Claude stared down and then ate a piece of the banana nut muffin. He took a while to swallow before speaking. With a choked reply, he said. "We argued the day before. Me and Becca. I never imagined that I would never see her again. It's truly not a good idea to stay angry with someone."

Don't let the sun go down while you are still angry.

That's one of the few bible verses I had learned over the years. I glanced at Eleanor. I knew she was almost finished writing a book that was loosely based on Rebecca's disappearance. But I wasn't sure if Claude was aware of this.

"Well, maybe I can help." I shifted my weight from one foot to the other. "I've been thinking about what to talk about next for the *Cold Justice Podcast*. People keep asking me if I'm going to do a new season." I paused. "Do you think it would be a good idea for me to discuss Rebecca's disappearance?"

Claude bit his lower lip before replying. "Joss, I'm not sure if that's such a good idea. I mean, I appreciate the thought, but Rebecca's case... it's different."

I placed my hand on my hips. "Different how?"

He hesitated, looking down at his hands. "Rebecca was acting off in the weeks leading up to her disappearance. I don't want you getting involved in anything dangerous."

"Dangerous?" I commented. "What exactly was Rebecca involved in?"

Claude sighed, his shoulders slumping. "You mean who was she involved with? You would have to talk to these people to get a podcast going, and I'm not sure if that's a good idea." He suddenly sat up straighter. "You're dating Detective Baez now. He might also have the same concerns as I do with you doing the podcast."

"Oh." I confessed with a blush. Andre and I met just as I'd launched my first podcast. He had some choice words about me pursuing my own investigation. Since then I'd been quiet and focused on developing our relationship.

But lately I've been itching to do something. To get back to my podcast. I didn't want to be a one hit wonder. I really wanted to pursue the truth in other cold cases too.

Claude interrupted my thoughts. "Maybe Detective Baez can find out about the status of Becca's investigation."

"Claude, if there were people around Rebecca that could have caused her harm, why didn't the police approach them instead of bothering you?"

He shrugged. "I guess I was an easier target."

"Oh no."

Claude and I turned to Eleanor. She hadn't been contributing to the conversation, but her face was paler than usual as she looked over at Claude.

"What's wrong?" I asked. "Did you find something?"

Eleanor clasped her hands across her chest. "It's all over social media. Some hiker and his dog found human remains."

Claude gripped the table so hard his knuckles turned white. With barely a whisper, he asked what I was sure we were all thinking. "Becca? Is it her?"

Could that possibly have been the message Andre received on his phone earlier? Was that where he was headed?

If this body really was Rebecca Montgomery, what happened to her? And why was she resurfacing now?

Tuesday, June 11, 10:53 a.m.

Claude didn't stay. And I couldn't blame him. Eleanor and I watched as he hurried from the café. He already looked troubled, but his face had grown pale like he was about to be sick.

Even though he'd left, I spoke in a low voice. "Do you think it's ..."

Eleanor nodded. "I can't explain why, but I think so. Rebecca Montgomery has been on my mind."

I raised an eyebrow. "Could it be because you're almost finished with the book?"

She flushed behind her oval framed glasses. Eleanor had been writing mystery novels for decades. I'd read some of them and often guessed incorrectly whodunit. She was a master at her craft. Over the years, her novels often took plots from real life, like the disappearance of Rebecca. Of course, Eleanor used fictional names. But from the way she described the plot, it had all the main characters including Claude.

Eleanor cleared her throat and drank a sip from her cup before answering me. "It's finished and with my editor. It won't come out for another eight months. But you're right. With all the research I had to do, I often wondered if the truth of her disappearance would finally come out. I know for many missing persons, that never happens."

I needed to get back behind the counter, but there was a lull in the café at the moment. We had at least thirty to forty minutes before the early lunch crowd trickled in, enough time for me to clean tables and restock the counter.

I took advantage of the few minutes to clean the surrounding tables. "So, did you get a sense if anyone had anything to do with Rebecca's disappearance? We know it wasn't Claude."

Eleanor's brows furrowed. "Of course not. They argued. From what I can remember, Rebecca argued with a lot of people. She had strong opinions and didn't mind making them known."

"I'd heard that about her. She was also an activist too, right?"

Eleanor sighed. "Yes. She used her artwork to highlight injustices. You know the community drew a lot of comfort from the mural outside the Sugar Creek Lofts."

I nodded. I was familiar with the mural since I spent a good bit of time at the Lofts. I'd started using the studio there with DJ Blaze over a year ago to record the *Cold Justice* podcast. My friend could no longer help me because he was serving time. I didn't want to think about all that happened last fall. It made me really sad. Even though I learned a lot from him, I wasn't sure if I could do the podcast on my own. Lately, I'd missed it. I loved talking to guests and hearing their insights. I received so many emails and comments of encouragement on social media but struggled with what to do for season two.

Now, I think I knew.

If Eleanor could write a book, why couldn't I pursue the cold case? It'd been three years and no one still had any clue what happened.

That might change today.

If the remains were indeed Rebecca Montgomery.

Chapter 2
Pursuing Mayhem

Tuesday, June 11, 6:12 p.m.

I locked the door after the last customer left. That customer happened to be Eleanor. She used the café as an office and, most days, was the last person to leave other than the staff. She whispered to me on the way out the door.

"If you want to pursue Rebecca's story for your podcast, I can share my research with you. I approached a few of the people in her life. Just beware. Some of them didn't want to talk to me, never even responded to my emails. But I'm also an older woman and couldn't relate to them. Even though it won't be easy, you might have a better chance at getting their attention."

"Thanks, Eleanor. I'd appreciate any insight you're willing to share." While I appreciated Eleanor's willingness to provide her research, I wanted to do my own digging. Still, it would be good to compare whatever I found with hers.

I shut the lights off around the café and headed into the back. Fay was in her office staring at her monitor. She looked up as I approached, and I knew something was wrong. I stopped mid-step, my heart fluttering in my chest. Fay was the strongest woman I knew, and the strongest emotions she showed were joy, annoyance and sometimes anger. Her red rimmed eyes with unshed tears alarmed me.

I rushed forward afraid something had happened with our precious café. "Fay, what's wrong? Is it Rick Nelson? Please don't tell me he has gotten his way."

Fay shook her head. "No, no. It's ..." She turned her monitor around to face me. "It's all over social media. Everyone is speculating that the remains found early this morning are Becca's."

I stepped forward to study the Facebook post. I'd seen this photo of Rebecca Montgomery many times. It was taken inside an art gallery. A bronze toned woman with a slim figure and large doe brown eyes, Rebecca had been stunning. At first glance, she appeared delicate, but the sharp, almost seductive look she gave the camera insinuated a fierceness beneath the surface.

She seemed to use her body like a canvas from head to toe. Long dreadlocks with purple and burgundy coloring at the ends stuck out from her head like Medusa. Her small frame was wrapped in a bright gold, off the shoulder jumpsuit. On one arm there was a distinct tattoo, but I couldn't tell what it was from where I stood.

I wondered if Andre knew about this. "Have the cops released a statement yet?"

Fay grabbed a tissue from her desk and blew her nose. "No. Our local *wanna-be- reporter* was down near the crime scene. He's spreading speculation all over his Instagram and TikTok. You know how social media can be. One person supposedly breaks the latest news and everyone else is picking it up and spreading it to their followers. It's all over every feed."

Fay's phone rang and she answered. "Excuse me, it's Joe."

Joe was Fay's boyfriend, so I stepped away to grab my phone from my pocket.

I knew who Fay was referring to and did a search.

Liam Holbrook.

A handsome man with vivid green eyes stared back from the profile picture. I clicked on his latest post on Instagram and a reel started playing.

Liam looked around before staring intently at the camera. He appeared to be inside his car, which is where he did a lot of his so-called reporting. Usually he did a lot of ranting.

"Breaking news, everyone. Liam here from *Shady Affairs*, and I've got some shocking updates for you. I've just received word that the police have discovered the remains of a body in Francis Marion State Forest. This is a developing story and details are still coming in, but you know how I like to stay on top of things."

He leaned closer to the camera as if he had a secret to share.

"Now, here's where things get interesting. My sources are telling me that there's speculation going around that the remains could belong to none other than Rebecca Montgomery, the artist who vanished without a trace three years ago. As many of you know, the anniversary of her disappearance was a few days ago. Invitations to the annual gala at the Ashford Art Gallery have already been sent out and yours truly has an invitation.

"In case you didn't know, Rebecca disappeared three days after the gala where her infamous mural, *Black Girl Magic* was revealed. She'd been known to be a difficult person, maybe even suffering from mental illness."

Liam closed his eyes as if in deep contemplation. When he opened them again, he looked into the camera, appearing sympathetic.

"I want to stress that this is all speculation at this point, and we won't know for sure until the authorities complete their investigation and identify the remains. But you can bet that I'll be following this story closely and bringing you updates as soon as I have them."

He smiled, his eyes bright like he was your best friend.

"In the meantime, I want to hear from you. What do you think about this latest development? Do you believe the remains could belong to Rebecca Montgomery? What theories do you have about her disappearance? Leave your comments below, and let's get the discussion going.

"As always, thanks for tuning in to *Shady Affairs*. Stay vigilant, my friends."

As usual with short reels, the video started back over, but I swiped my screen to close the app.

The social media celebrity lived here in Charleston and frequented the café. While he wasn't a regular like Eleanor, Liam usually came in once or twice a week to order a black coffee and flirt shamelessly with the baristas, including me.

I'd worked at Hooters at one point in my life, a low point where I just needed a job. So males trying to shoot their shot was nothing new to me. Liam was one of those with looks, but no manners that appealed to a sensible woman.

Fay didn't like him at all. He'd posted a bad review about the café on his social media a few summers back. She didn't have the staff then that she had now, so the lines were long, increasing the wait time. But people who were loyal and loved Fay stuck around. Apparently, Liam was one of those who got impatient. Like a lot of people who used their platforms on social media to vent, Liam made sure all of his 50,000 followers at the time knew about his experience.

It didn't hurt the café. Most of the people that followed Liam weren't even in the Charleston area. Now boasting almost 100,000 followers, Liam popped up on reels and TikToks spreading opinion more so than fact.

While she didn't want to, Fay offered him a free coffee, which he gladly took. He at least posted about his experience, but he'd still never gotten back into Fay's good graces.

In fact, he was dangerously close to getting banned from the café. A few months ago while covering a city council meeting, Liam painted Fay in a bad light, stating she was holding up progress for Sugar Creek by leading the charge against the proposed development of the area. It surprised me that he would be on Rick Nelson's side and made me suspicious of his intentions. Seeing the type of sponsors Liam pulled, I wouldn't

A LATTE MAYHEM

be surprised if he'd taken some money from the car salesman trying to get into the development world.

After my podcast launched last fall, one day Liam asked me if I would produce another season. I was surprised he'd been paying attention. I didn't know if he was being nice or checking me out as competition. The man used all forms of media to spread his influence and opinions under his Shady Affairs brand which included a podcast too. I wouldn't call it true crime since Liam reported on a hodgepodge of topics, mainly gossip.

Even though he was a customer, I heeded warnings not to share anything with him. Liam could be charming, but he was always hunting down the latest story. And he'd been accused of twisting words out of context. It was all about the algorithm to him. With his large social media following, I certainly didn't need the kind of hassle that came from Liam's tribe of trolls. If I did decide to move forward with Rebecca's cold case, I knew to stay away from him.

I wondered if anyone would pay attention to my podcast. This was a really big case. Everybody wanted to get to the truth. Both traditional media and every blogger turned journalist. Not to mention other true crime podcasters.

Fay had finished her conversation with Joe and called me back to the office. "Joss, you can head out if you need to. Joe will be by to pick me up."

Like me, Fay refused to purchase a new vehicle. I was sure she could afford one, but she loved her white Nissan Altima. It had been in the shop with transmission issues for a few days.

I glanced at my phone. "I probably should head on. Andre is fixing dinner tonight."

Fay smiled. "I'm so happy for you. You finally snagged a good one."

I blushed. "I like to think so. You know I've never asked you this, but did you know her too? Rebecca Montgomery?"

Fay snatched a tissue off her desk and blotted her eyes. "Oh my goodness, yes. She was a buddy of mine. But she was Becca to me and Claude. We've known each other since elementary school. Becca never fit the mold that people tried to put her in. She always stuck up for others like Claude, who was a nerdy little beanpole."

"What? Our Claude?"

Fay grinned. "Yes. Claude was a late bloomer. Somewhere around our senior year, he started wearing contacts and filled out some. He and Becca went to our senior prom together. I will have to dig out my yearbook one of these days so you can see us all back then." Fay sighed and leaned back in her desk chair. "Becca was a regular here at the café before you started. Loved her vanilla latte."

"I wish I'd known her. What was she like?"

Fay's eyes took on a faraway look, as if she were lost in a memory. "Becca was a free spirit, always sketching in that notebook of hers. She had a heart of gold, constantly looking out for others. Out of all the artists I knew, she was the one who believed her art should draw people's eyes to the evil in the world. Before she disappeared, I was hoping she'd do a mural in the back of the café. We talked about it a lot. She'd proposed doing something in that back area that we used for Friday Night Jams."

"That would have been beautiful."

The café already felt like walking into one's home. There were a scattering of homey tables and chairs in the center. Booths lined the side walls, and the back of the café had couches and chairs that were great for reading and even studying. On the second Friday of each month, that area was transformed into a stage with chairs and tables all around for musicians to spoken word artists to share their talents.

"What about her relationship with Claude? I know they were close and it really hurt him that the police approached him about her disappearance. Today, he especially seemed not like himself."

Fay's expression turned somber. "I'm sure it's the anniversary of Becca's disappearance. Believe it or not, Claude used to take better care of himself. He used to keep his hair cut and wore a goatee. Life hit him pretty hard after his father died. Then Becca disappeared. He'd been head over heels in love with that girl since middle school. Unfortunately, Becca only ever saw him as a brother. He used to say she didn't want him because he was white, but that wasn't true at all."

I frowned. "What do you mean?"

Fay rolled her eyes. "Becca fell for a rich white guy named Ethan Turner. He owns the tech startup, Synaptic. It's supposed to specialize in AI tools for artists and musicians. Anyway, Ethan hired her to design a mural for his building. Next thing you know, they started dating. He's a good looking guy, but I didn't think he was her type."

I frowned. "Was she dating Ethan at the time of her disappearance? Did the cops bother him like they did Claude?"

Fay shook her head, her expression troubled. "I heard he was questioned but he had a better alibi than Claude. Unfortunately, our dear forgetful friend spends too much time alone with his work and no one could corroborate his story."

I shook my head. "Poor Claude. He hasn't been able to catch a break."

Claude was attacked last fall and still had some PSTD from that incident, though he liked to underplay it.

Fay stood and plucked an envelope from the shelf above her desk. She handed it to me. "If you want to meet Ethan, his company is a major sponsor of this year's gala at the Ashford Art Gallery. I got an invitation, but I wasn't sure I wanted to go this year. I visit the gallery a few times a year to see the last mural Becca painted."

I pulled a stock white card from the envelope with embossed text.

The Annual Gala at Ashford Art Gallery
presented by Synaptic
Saturday, July 6
7:00 p.m.

"Wow! This is fancy! Why wouldn't you go? Everyone knows you are a force in the art community."

Fay's eyes again filled with tears, before she looked away. "It feels wrong to celebrate when we still don't know what happened to Becca. She disappeared three days after the gala three years ago, you know. And she was the star of the gala that year."

Fay pointed to the photo on her computer monitor. "It's where that photo was taken. No one knew she would disappear days later. I wish you could have met her. She would have liked you. Both of you have that understated spunk that people don't see coming."

I cringed. "I wouldn't call myself an activist like you and Rebecca."

Fay smiled. "I've always told you there are great things that you're gonna be doing. Kicking off the podcast and bringing attention to your grandfather's unsolved murder last year, that was just the beginning."

I pulled out my phone and snapped a photo of the invitation. I wanted to check out more about the gala later. I returned the card to the envelope and handed it back to Fay. "Do you think the police will bother Claude again?"

Fay scrunched her nose. "I don't doubt that they will. Becca's older sister, Olivia hasn't given up and she was the main person telling the police about Claude and her sister's argument. We all grew up together. I don't see how she thinks Claude did something. But then again, Olivia never understood her own sister."

"Are you saying they didn't get along?"

Fay smirked. "Not really. They were too opposite. Becca was artistic and Olivia was conservative. Becca attracted people to her like a butterfly to a flower. Her sister can be rough around the edges, almost rude sometimes. I never told Becca this, but I felt like Olivia was jealous of her. Nothing Becca did ever pleased her. I guess her going after Claude is more about her own guilt for not appreciating her younger sister."

"That's a shame. Suppose I can help Claude out. If reporters catch wind that he's back on the police's radar, they won't leave him alone. Who would be in his corner trying to prove his innocence? What if I can help him out with the *Cold Justice* podcast?"

"You are a really good friend, Joss." Fay frowned. "But do you think Andre is going to like you poking around in this case, especially if that body really is Becca?"

I felt annoyed. "I'm sure he won't like it, but I want to give a voice to the people who loved Rebecca. There can't be any harm in that. Would you want me to interview you?"

Fay looked at me for a few minutes. "I don't know, Joss. I feel like I need to keep a low profile and concentrate on keeping the café from being snatched away by Rick Nelson. I haven't been able to go to the gala all these years. It's so hard." She picked up the invitation. "But if you want to go to the gala, I will see if I can get you tickets and come with you. It might be a good outing for you and Andre. And I can see if I can convince Joe."

I grinned. "I doubt we will have to do too much convincing to our guys. Joe is going to love seeing you dressed up, and I haven't gone anywhere more formal than a wedding with Andre."

Fay laughed. "Sounds like a plan. Maybe we can find some people who will be willing to talk to you on your podcast." Then her face sobered. "Promise me you'll be careful as you move forward. We know Claude is innocent, but somebody out there knows what happened to Becca. I have always had this feeling that it was someone she knew or someone she upset."

I squeezed her hand. "I will. Look, I better go. I don't need Andre looking for me."

Fay grinned. "Ohhh, I love it that you got a man that can cook."

"Me too, girl!"

I headed out, making sure the door locked behind me. My mind was moving in all kinds of directions. I figured there were going to be a lot of people interested in investigating Rebecca's disappearance. I just wanted my little podcast to help keep a friend from going to jail for something he didn't do.

A LATTE MAYHEM

Tuesday, June 11, 7:05 p.m.

My heart raced as I pulled my bright red Honda Civic in front of Andre's townhouse. I always felt a tingle of excitement being around him. From the outside, some folks might say that we had a slow burn relationship. I was attracted to him the first time I met him last September. He'd dropped hints that he felt the same. Despite that attraction, I soon learned trying to get involved with Detective Andre Baez wasn't easy. We didn't go out on our first date until the end of October.

A homicide detective in the Charleston Police Department, he transferred here last summer from working cold cases in Charlotte, North Carolina. The murder of a shop owner next to Sugar Creek Café brought us together. I'd found the deceased woman, who, unfortunately, had been a descendant of one of my grandfather's murderers. The timing wasn't great for me since I'd just launched the podcast covering my grandfather's murder.

It was not an ideal way to start a relationship.

We went out exactly three times last year, mainly dinner dates, roughly once a month. It wasn't until New Year's Eve that we actually kissed and made it more official. I have to say that was the longest I'd ever gone before kissing a guy. I was always the girl who jumped hard and fast with men. Not that there had been many men in my life. I'd moved in with two past boyfriends, one out of rebellion to my mom's griping. The other felt like a good thing to do at the time.

Now in my late twenties, I'd learned I wanted something that was going to be real. I didn't like how empty I felt after getting my heart broken. There was nothing quite like packing up your things and leaving a guy you once thought was the one. So despite my longing for more with Detective Andre Baez, the slower pace was what we needed, what I needed.

I wasn't sure when I decided to pursue being celibate, perhaps when Andre told me he'd been practicing celibacy for over a year. I'd never met a man who was set on getting to know me. Sometimes, I felt overwhelmed, scared. Andre seemed too good to be true. But other times, the nature of his profession reminded me of how tenuous our relationship could be.

I prayed it lasted. I really did like him. A lot!

I climbed out of my car and walked up the pathway. Andre had been promising for several weeks that he would cook for me. With the unpredictability of his vocation, many dates were broken, but I understood that his work was important. Sometimes, Andre dropped hints about what he was working on. And sometimes, he didn't. I hoped he would tell me more about why he ran off earlier and if it had to do with the body found earlier today.

Andre opened the door. Despite the dark circles beneath them, his eyes and smile appeared bright. The weariness didn't diminish his handsome features. "Hey, babe, come on in," he said, stepping aside to let me enter.

Once inside, he reached down and hugged me. I melted in his arms for what seemed like a few minutes before pulling back. "You look like you've had a long day."

He grimaced. "You could say that. I'm sure you're tired too from being on your feet all day. Grab a seat. Dinner will be ready in a bit."

My feet were actually pretty worn down. I removed my trusty sneakers before I walked into the living room. Andre's home, with its plush leather couch and chairs, was always warm and inviting. The soft lighting made it feel romantic. I wasn't sure if that was Andre's intent or if my hormones were stirring. Despite our resolve to not pursue physical intimacy, sometimes my brain didn't follow suit.

I sank down on the couch. It felt good to stretch my toes. Andre's large flat screen television was on but the volume was low. I reached for the remote when I saw the news story about the remains in the woods.

Unlike the report I saw on social media, a television news reporter stood in front of a wooded area. Behind her, a deputy hung yellow crime scene tape.

"I'm here at Francis Marion State Forest where the skeletal remains of a body was discovered by a hiker and his dog this afternoon about a mile off the Palmetto Trail. While we wait for authorities to identify the remains, police are combing the area for evidence. This is a developing story and we'll bring you more details as they emerge. Back to you in the studio."

Andre called out. "Dinner is ready."

I reluctantly put the remote on the coffee table and tried hard to concentrate on dinner. I took a seat at the dining room table as Andre served up two plates of rigatoni. Andre had a passion for all kinds of food, but his specialty was definitely Italian cuisine. Biting into the warm slice of ciabatta bread drizzled with olive oil and oregano, I forgot all about the questions swimming in my head from the news broadcast.

"Mmmm, this is so good!" I oozed my pleasure with no shame. Andre was a much better cook than me.

He laughed. "Glad your taste buds approve."

We ate in silence. The only sound that could be heard was the clink of silverware against ceramic. Finally, I couldn't take it anymore. "Where did you run off to this morning? Did it have anything to do with the body found this morning? Actually sounds like it was more like skeletal remains since it's been out there awhile. Who found it?"

Andre held up his fork. "Whoa, whoa! Slow down." He shook his head. "I was kind of hoping to enjoy our dinner together."

My face grew warm. "Sorry! But you've heard all the rumors about who it could be right?"

Andre hesitated, his eyes flickering away from mine. "Yes, but I'm not sure why people assumed it could be Rebecca Montgomery. Many women have gone missing. The remains could be anyone."

I eyed him. "But you know something."

Andre leaned back in his seat. "I shouldn't be talking to you about this, but it will probably make the news in the morning. Because of the uproar to identify the remains, the coroner rushed the lab results on this one. Highly unusual, but the dental records matched. It's Rebecca Montgomery."

I felt like I'd been punched in the gut. Hearing it confirmed made it all too real. "So you're going to investigate what happened? You know, talk to all the people in her life?"

Andre drank a swig of tea before answering. "That's my job."

"Would you be upset if I decided to focus on Rebecca Montgomery for the second season of my podcast?"

Andre's eyes snapped back to mine, his expression fierce. "Absolutely not, Joss. This is an active investigation. I can't have you interfering."

A ripple of irritation rose, but I tamped it down. I expected this. I leaned forward. "I'm not going to interfere. There are plenty of reporters out there who will want to get all the information they can get. That's not what I'm doing. I want to offer a platform to people who want to talk about Rebecca. People who loved her. Besides, people might open up to me in a way they won't with the police. Suppose I can help you find the truth?"

Andre shook his head. "Joss, this isn't like your last podcast. There's still a lot of unanswered questions and we don't know how Rebecca died. If you start poking around, you could put yourself in real danger. You have to let me handle this."

I knew Andre was a good detective, and that he would do everything in his power to solve this case. But I also knew there was something I could do too.

"Andre, I'm not going to get in your way. I promise. My podcast will be a forum for folks to talk, like it was for my first season."

Andre held his head down and sighed. "You've already made up your mind. Why did you even ask me?"

I frowned. "Because it's important to me that you are okay with it."

We stared at each other across the table.

Andre broke the silence. "Promise me you'll be careful. And if you start to feel like you're in over your head or someone is giving bad vibes, come to me."

"Of course." I grinned as I started gathering our plates. "Now, since you cooked dinner, let me cleanup for you. The night is still young."

Andre chuckled. "I see what you're doing. Trying to get my mind off your podcast by tempting me."

"I hope it's working." I said purposely swishing my hips as I entered the kitchen.

After last season, I wasn't sure I wanted to continue with the podcast. But now, as I watched the steamy, sudsy water rise in the kitchen sink, my passion sparked once again at the prospect of starting a new season.

Andre, reaching his hands around my waist, lit up a different type of passion.

Chapter 3
Groundwork Begins

Wednesday, June 12, 9:05 a.m.

I had most Wednesdays off, which I really needed. I'd worked two Saturdays in a row this month due to staff changes. The café remained open six days a week and closed on Sundays. Fay kept a small staff that consisted of me, as assistant manager, and a few other baristas. Another barista, Briana Jones, worked whenever she was in town. These days, she traveled a good bit, taking on singing gigs across the Southeast. Other staff members from nearby local colleges rotated in and out.

Since I'd pretty much decided to pursue the topic of Rebecca Montgomery's disappearance for the next season of my podcast, today would be my first day of deep research. I lingered in bed, stressing. Would people even want to talk to me? Eleanor said it was hard for her to get people to talk to her and she was a successful author.

Before I threw back my covers, I looked over to check on my roommate, a tuxedo cat. She stretched her paws out and mewed at me. I rubbed Minnie's head. The smallest and only female cat in the house had claimed me as her human.

Honored by her affectionate head rub, I told her. "We have a busy day ahead."

Since moving into the house with my grandmother, I'd learned to get used to having a feline on my bed. When I came in last night, Minnie greeted me at the door. Her brother, Mickey, also a tuxedo cat, strutted up right behind her. The oldest cat, an eleven year old orange cat perfectly named, Ginger, peeked at me from the top of the staircase. With only the lamp on in the living room, I'd guessed my grandmother had headed to bed early. Her cats made it a habit to wait up for me, making sure I arrived home at a decent hour.

Today was also hair wash day. My thick curly hair needed tackling alongside my research. But first – coffee. The cat leaped off the bed as I headed downstairs.

When I entered the kitchen, I could see my grandmother outside in her garden. The big orange tabby lay on the windowsill outside and peered inside at me. I poured coffee in my Snoopy mug, a gift from my dad many years ago and went to the back door. Stepping out onto the porch, the humidity hit me like I was walking through some type of force field. I almost would have liked a tall glass of iced coffee instead.

"Have you been out here long?" I asked with concern. Louise was a spunky seventy-four, but she needed to be careful out in this heat.

My grandmother grinned at me, the floppy hat shielding her blue eyes from the sun. "Only about an hour. I'll be ready to go in soon. This sun isn't playing and it's not even mid-morning yet."

I laughed. "That's Charleston for you. I'm going back inside."

"I'm right behind you." My grandmother cackled. "Let me get you some breakfast."

"Oh, you don't have to do that."

Louise's eyes crinkled. "You are up early and you've worked long hours at the café. I know Andre fed you last night. Now, let me help get some meat on those bones."

I felt like I had plenty of meat on my bones. Being skinny had never been my thing, but I knew the older women in my life showed love with food. So I sat at the table as my grandmother grabbed her mixing bowls. I had to admit, she made some delicious, homemade buttermilk pancakes.

How my relationship had developed over the years with my grandmother Louise Hopkins was interesting. Louise was forced to give up my mom when she was in her late teens. It was pretty taboo at the time for a white woman to be involved with a Black man, my grandfather, August Manning. Having a child out of wedlock was definitely not going to be allowed. My mother researched finding her biological mom but was turned away by Louise's deceased husband.

For years, my mother felt the sting of that rejection, not knowing that Louise never knew her only daughter had been trying to reach out to her. After my dad died, my small family splintered and I got it in my head to reach out to Louise. Then I discovered the history of my grandparents' relationship.

My mother wasn't too happy about me exploring her biological parents through my podcast at first. And even though she didn't understand the medium, Louise loved it and jumped at an opportunity to talk about what had been on her mind for years.

I figured I would get her take on my new topic as I doused my pancakes with maple syrup. "Do you know anything about Rebecca Montgomery? I think her case could be the subject for the next season of my podcast."

My grandmother thoughtfully chewed her pancakes before answering. "Oh my, is that the young lady that went missing? They said that could be her body they found yesterday morning. What did Andre say?"

I nodded. "He said the dental records were a match."

My grandmother raised her eyebrow. "More than likely she was murdered, right? Would that be safe for you to investigate?"

I admitted. "I'm not trying to do the police's job. I'm thinking my angle would be to hear what friends and family have to say about her. You know, make her story more human."

Louise smiled. "Well, if anyone can do that, you can. You were able to share your grandfather's story with a lot of people."

"The hardest part is going to be getting people to want to talk to me. I'm going to look into it more while I tackle my hair today." I scrolled on my phone to where I'd snapped a photo of Fay's invitation. "The Ashford Art Gallery. Do you know anything about it or where it's located?"

My grandmother's face lit up. "Yes, I know that place. It's owned by an old family here in Charleston. The Ashfords. I remember when the gallery opened. It was a big deal. Goodness, that's been almost twenty years."

"The owner's name is Vivian Ashford. Do you know anything about her?"

Louise rubbed her chin. "I know she's not originally from here. Well, a lot of people move to Charleston. But Vivian was born and raised in London, England. Her husband, Mitchell Ashford, died quite a few years ago. But he was from old money. As I understand, Vivian wasn't that poor herself."

"Sounds like an interesting person. I wonder if she knew Rebecca well. That photo they keep showing of her was taken inside the art gallery. Then she disappeared a few days later."

My grandmother placed her hand over her chest. "Oh my! I'm sure Vivian knows all the artists in Charleston and beyond. That painting I have in the living room with the Charleston Harbor was purchased from her gallery."

"I love that painting. I need to check out the gallery. But, before I try booking anyone, I need to talk to Claude first. He's really the whole reason why I want to do this."

My grandmother shook her head. "That poor young man. I remember when they kept bringing his name up in the news. I certainly hope the police don't bother him again. It didn't seem like he did anything to me."

"I agree. Let's hope he trusts our friendship enough to talk to me."

A LATTE MAYHEM

Wednesday, June 12, 11:38 a.m.

I washed my hair and decided to give myself a much needed steam treatment. Sometimes, it felt like a good portion of my income went to hair products, but the steam cap I invested in was worth it. It was almost like being at the spa. My grandmother had gone next door to chat with our next door neighbor Eugeena Patterson-Jones, so I had the house to myself. Well, at least me and my feline housemates.

I got to work on my MacBook. This was the part I loved. Research. There was no doubt in my mind that I would forge ahead with this season's topic for the podcast. Though I never had any dreams of journalism, my love for crime shows had taught me the art of investigation.

Surprisingly, Rebecca Montgomery's social media profiles remained active. I wondered if her sister kept the posts going. From the few photos I could find from Rebecca's Instagram, I gauged the two sisters were definitely different. Where Rebecca's fashion style reflected her free spirit, more bohemian and eclectic, Olivia Montgomery seemed more reserved and conservative. I clicked on her profile to learn more about her.

The first thing I observed about Olivia's Instagram account, it seemed dedicated to finding her sister. There were more posts of the sisters, but many repeat posts of Rebecca in that last photo she took at the gallery. Where Olivia seemed dedicated to finding out what happened to her sister, I needed to know more about her. I clicked on a link from her bio that led to Olivia's LinkedIn profile. That was one social media platform I had never signed up for. Networking wasn't really my thing.

After a quick perusal, I discovered Olivia was a lawyer, but not the kind who did criminal or even civil cases. Olivia specialized in business law. Even here, there were posts about Rebecca. One post intrigued me, it appeared to be an interview. The link bounced me over to a YouTube channel that belonged to the local news station.

I recognized the morning anchor, Daniella Bradley. Olivia sat in a chair facing the reporter, her salt and pepper hair in a sharp bob. She looked austere and stately in a black suit, like she was in mourning. Which could have been possible, the date of the interview was a year ago, the second anniversary of Rebecca's disappearance. I turned up the volume so I could hear.

"I'm frustrated by the lack of progress to find my sister." Olivia spoke candidly, sharing stories about her younger sister's life. "She'd always been an artist. Art gave her life, kept her out of depression when our mom died."

As I watched the interview, I wondered if Olivia would be willing to talk to me. She probably knew her sister better than anyone else.

Olivia told the reporter, "We'd been estranged for some time before her disappearance." Her eyes filled with tears as she looked away from the camera. "Sorry."

Daniella beckoned someone over with a box of tissues. She waited until Olivia composed herself then said, "Tell us more about your relationship after your mother died."

Olivia wiped her eyes. "My mom lost her battle with breast cancer about five years ago. In a way, I'm glad my mother didn't have to experience all of this. My sister and I are ... were different. I didn't always understand her passion for art. I didn't see how it could sustain her, but she proved me wrong. I'm proud of her success."

Daniella said, "Your sister was quite active in speaking out about many social injustices and even used her artwork to express her thoughts."

Olivia smiled. "Rebecca always stood up for what she believed in, even when it made her unpopular. She had a way of shining light on the truth, no matter how uncomfortable it might be."

I paused the video. That made me think of Claude's words yesterday. He thought Rebecca had come across something dangerous. Why did he think that? Claude had argued with his friend before she disappeared, but what did they argue about?

I focused on finishing up my wash day routine by twisting my hair into two pigtails. The warmer it got, the more likely I'd opt for air drying my hair versus blow drying. And I had a limited amount of time on my day off.

I needed to know what happened in the days prior to Rebecca's disappearance.

I pulled on a silk-lined baseball cap to protect my hair, and then wrote my grandmother a note. Even though she had a phone, she refused to read texts. Louise preferred to use a phone for what it was made for – talking. The sun beat down on my head, making me grateful for the hat.

Claude often disappeared and withdrew from the public eye. Sometimes he would be deep into a painting, or even several paintings at the same time. I had a feeling he would be hiding out even more so now. I decided against texting him to let him know I was coming since he often forgot to charge his phone.

Ten minutes later, I pulled into the parking lot of Sugar Creek Lofts, better known as the Lofts. The building used to be a textile mill. Owned by the Nelson family, the building was renovated and transformed into an art center by the matriarch. Many artists and musicians rented spaces inside. Claude was one of a few who rented and lived inside a studio apartment on the second floor.

Before heading toward the entrance, I strolled around to the side of the building which faced a park. There were children playing, so it was noisier than usual for a Wednesday. School had closed for the summer.

I stopped to look at the mural on the side of the building. I'd viewed it many times. A striking tribute to the Emmanuel Nine, the nine Black church members who were tragically killed in the Charleston church shooting, the mural was a vibrant explosion of color and emotion against the red brick of the building.

In the center of the mural was a stylized portrait of Mother Emanuel AME Church, its white façade and tall steeple rendered in bold, graphic lines. Surrounding the church were nine doves, each one unique in its colors and patterns, representing the nine lives lost. The doves were painted in a swirl of bright hues—deep purples, vivid blues, fiery oranges—their wings outstretched as if in flight.

Interwoven among the doves were the words, "Love is always stronger than hate."

At the base of the mural, a crowd of figures stood hand in hand, their faces turned up toward the church and the doves. They were painted in shades of brown and black, a diverse representation of the Charleston community coming together in solidarity and mourning.

I wasn't sure why, but today I was struck by the power of the image as a whole. Once again, I wish I'd known the artist. Fay, Claude and many others were blessed to have known Rebecca while she was alive.

Blaze had given me his key card since he could no longer assist me with the podcast. He'd paid in advance for the usage of the studio. While I was still solidifying plans for what to do next with the podcast, at least I had access to the recording studio located off to the left of the entrance for awhile longer. The door buzzed and the entry door opened for me with a click.

I passed the shaded windows of the recording studio and headed toward the dark wooden staircase that led up to

A LATTE MAYHEM

Claude's studio apartment. Hand gripping the banister, I stopped abruptly at the bottom step.

Voices traveled down from upstairs.

One of the voices was an angry Claude.

Chapter 4
Vultures Circling

Wednesday, June 12, 1:34 p.m.

I hesitated trying to figure out who the other voice belonged to. It didn't take long.

"I have nothing to say to you, Liam."

I rolled my eyes. I'd arrived in time to save my friend from Liam Holbrook. I sprinted up the stairs to find Claude looking even more disheveled than usual. His man bun flopped to the side.

Claude caught sight of me coming and relief washed over his blue eyes.

I hurried over to the door with my fists balled. "Hey, Claude, is everything okay?"

Liam spun around, his eyes wide behind his Harry Potter looking glasses. I'd seen Liam on many occasions at the café. He wore his hair long in the front, often with one side hanging over his glasses. He reached up to brush his hair back as if to be sure he could see me better.

I stepped forward. "Hello, Liam."

Liam's eyes widened in recognition. "Hey, aren't you the girl from the café?"

Girl! I was a fully grown woman. Before I could respond, Claude intervened. He stepped across the threshold of his door toward Liam.

Two against one.

Liam had the decency to step back.

Claude growled, "I'm warning you, if you don't leave now, I'll—"

"Call the police." I interjected. We needed to get this vulture out of here. And I didn't want Claude to say something he would regret. I put my hand on my hip and glared at the man. "How did you get in here anyway?"

"He tricked me." Claude stated. "Claimed he had a package for me."

I sucked in a breath. That wasn't cool. It wasn't safe either. It could have been anybody. Claude was definitely not paying attention.

Liam scoffed, his eyes narrowing. "You're not going to call the police. Besides, the police are not your friends, Claude. They'll come bother you about being the last person to see Rebecca alive. Again." He shrugged as if he was all knowing. "I'm trying to help."

No, that's what I was planning to do.

My intentions were a lot more pure than this man.

I jabbed my finger at him. "Once Claude tells the police how you snuck your way inside private property, they are only going to be looking at you. I know the type of security required to get in here and I will be his witness."

Liam glared back at me before surrendering. He held up his hands. "Okay, okay, I'll go. I will leave you and your bodyguard alone. But you will need to talk to me sometime, Claude."

We both watched Liam trudge down the staircase. Once I heard the outer door close downstairs, I glanced over at Claude ready to scold him for not paying attention. All the security in this place and he let the enemy inside.

Before I could let him have it, weariness replaced the anger on his face. Claude looked like he hadn't slept in days. With dark circles under his eyes, the pain and frustration etched on his face made my heart go out to him. Unfortunately, Liam wouldn't be the only one trying to bother him. I wondered if I should say anything to him myself.

I placed a comforting hand on his arm. "Are you okay? You've got to be careful. I thought there were cameras that you could look at to see who's buzzing the door."

He groaned. "I know. He had on a brown cap, and his head was down. You know I order packages all the time. I didn't even look to see if there was an emblem on the stupid hat. I appreciate you showing up when you did. I'm so on edge right now. Did you come to see me?"

"I did. Are you okay with some company?"

"Sure. Warning. The place is a mess."

I couldn't recall when Claude's place was ever not messy. I followed him into his studio apartment which was one big room with a ladder leading up to where Claude slept. The entire bottom floor consisted of shelves and tables of painting supplies. In a corner near the window was a small kitchenette. His living room area consisted of an old couch that Claude had kept when his dad passed and a wood coffee table that had seen better days.

I knew his father's house was located down the street from Eleanor. Instead of staying in the home where he grew up, Claude chose to be here.

A LATTE MAYHEM

In some ways, I could understand why Claude chose not to live at his father's house. I imagine there were painful memories with both parents deceased.

When I moved out of the apartment with my ex-boyfriend, I had a choice to return home or go live with my newly discovered grandmother. I chose Louise's place. She was lonely and I wanted to get to know her. And, my mom and I didn't get along. Some of that was due to my choosing to shack up with my ex-boyfriend against her advice. When things went sour with Blaze, my mom's I-told-you-so was the last thing I wanted to hear.

There was a time when things were cool between us, but when my dad passed, our small family unit lost its closeness. My brother communicated when it seemed convenient for him, which was very little.

So, sometimes going home wasn't possible.

Claude looked at me. "You want coffee?"

"Sure. I was hoping we could talk." I followed him into the kitchenette. For a small area, there were several modern appliances, like Claude's bean to cup super-automatic espresso machine. I commented, "That's even fancier than what we have at the café."

He laughed. "Of my many bad habits, consuming coffee is a favorite. Fay got me sold on the Ethiopian blend that she uses."

"Ah, yeah. That's one of the premium flavors."

Claude cleared a space off the breakfast nook setup in the corner. "I'm sorry for the mess. I haven't had much motivation to clean lately."

I waved away his apology. "No worries. I'm glad you could see me." As the coffee brewed, I looked around and spotted a portrait of Rebecca, her vibrant eyes seemed to follow me. "That's new?"

Claude looked over to where I pointed. His face grew red and he quickly glanced away. "Yeah, I've been working on that one for a while."

"It's beautiful." And I wasn't just saying that. Claude was truly a talented artist.

He poured a steaming cup of coffee into a College of Charleston mug. With a puzzled look on his face, he placed the mug in front of me. I wrapped my hands around the mug grateful for the warmth. Nerves ate at me as I broached the subject that brought me here.

He sat down across from me. "Are you okay?"

I smiled not realizing I appeared nervous. "Yeah. I need to run something by you to get your thoughts."

A LATTE MAYHEM

A wariness crossed his face. "I think I know what it is."

"Oh? Yeah, I guess you do. I briefly mentioned the possibility yesterday. I'm settled on concentrating on Rebecca's disappearance for the next season of the podcast. I'm hoping you might be willing to be my first interview."

Claude's eyes widened. "Joss, I don't know. The police were all over me a few years back. They treated me like a suspect."

I noticed a slight tremor in his hands so I reached out and covered his hand with mine. "I know, Claude. And I'm sorry you had to go through that. But I can help tell your side of the story. You know me and I hope you can trust me."

Claude pulled his hand away. "What if talking about it puts me back in the crosshairs? I'm already getting hounded by reporters or wanna be reporters like that Liam fellow."

I nodded. "I understand, Claude. And you're right, everybody is going to be hounding you. Here I am doing the same."

I shouldn't have come.

My excitement dissipated in the silence.

As we sat quietly, I peeked at Claude. His eyes had slid to Rebecca's portrait. "Will you reveal the new painting?"

Claude hesitated for a moment. "I worked on it more for me. To remember her."

"Have you ever had your artwork featured at the Ashford Art Gallery?"

Claude shook his head. "No. But I've met her, the owner. Vivian Ashford. She's reached out to me, but I kind of stick to featuring my art in Fay's café. Besides, I don't like how she's associated with Ethan Turner."

I leaned in. "Rebecca was dating him. Did the cops question him like they did you?"

Claude sulked. "Not enough. Probably because he's rich and had lawyers at his beck and call. I really wish Becca had never gotten involved with him. She deserved so much better."

"Do you think he had anything to do with her disappearance?"

Claude stood and started pacing. "I don't know, but she didn't want anything to do with him that night at the gala."

"How so?"

He stood in front of the canvas. "I saw them argue and she walked away from him. There was this look on his face like this woman had some nerve embarrassing him."

I got up and joined him at the painting. Up close, the portrait was half-colored, but Rebecca's eyes stared back from the canvas.

Was this how Claude remembered her? With haunted eyes.

In a low voice, I asked. "Did you think she was in danger being around Ethan?"

He sighed and placed both hands on the sides of his face. "I'm not going to lie. I didn't like the guy. Still don't. I'm biased though. I'd been in love with Becca my whole life and she chose someone like *him*."

Claude shook his head and turned from the painting. "Something was off with her the entire time she dated him. I know I wasn't the only person who noticed it. Maybe it had to do with him or someone else." He turned to me. "You're my friend and I trust you. If anyone can tell the world about Becca you can. So, let's do it. I'm tired of being quiet about it, and I don't want the cops on my back or people whispering about me behind my back."

Relief washed over me. This was going to happen after all.

Thursday, June 13, 8:32 p.m.

I didn't waste time pulling together my interview questions for Claude. Scared he would change his mind, I set up a recording time with him on Wednesday afternoon in the studio at the Lofts. The equipment was a little intimidating without DJ Blaze, my audio engineer from the first season. But I remembered a few things, like how to hit record on the mics and save the .wav file.

Editing would be a whole other thing.

So I didn't pull out my hair, I called my good friend DJ Nyla B. Usually, she was booked for all kinds of events this time of year. Thankfully, Fay let me leave the café a bit early so I could meet Nyla at the recording studio at six thirty. I made sure to bring coffee, sandwiches and pastries. Without a budget, and being a long way from getting sponsors for the podcast, I did my best to accommodate my friend.

"This is golden, girl." Nyla said. "I'm so happy you're starting up your podcast again. I was afraid with everything that went down with Blaze that you wouldn't pursue it anymore."

Based on a series of events last fall, my ex-boyfriend, Blaze, had to go away for a while. His absence upset me in a way I hadn't imagined and in some ways left me in limbo about continuing the podcast. He helped me launch the first season.

"I had a lot to think about and needed to figure out what was next. Focusing on my grandfather's murder had been on my mind for so long."

Nyla grinned. "You are a full-fledged podcaster. You know I had an interview at the radio station with Rebecca Montgomery before she disappeared."

I lifted an eyebrow. "So you met her before? When was this?"

Nyla nodded. "I'd seen her around at events over the years. But her publicist booked Rebecca as a guest on the morning show a few days before the big gala held at Ashford Art Gallery. She was really cool and down to earth. I liked her vibe."

"I've heard nothing but good things about her. I wished I'd met her. Did you get any sense that something might have been wrong?"

Nyla closed her eyes as if trying to think back. "No. Not really. I remember she seemed annoyed. Not at me or about doing the interview. Her publicist was really bossy. There was a lot of tension there."

I frowned. "Her publicist was at the interview?"

Nyla nodded. "Yeah! I got the sense that the publicist really pushed Rebecca to do the interview. It was like the publicist thought if she didn't show up with her, that Rebecca would have bailed."

"Do you remember her name?"

Nyla shook her head. "Not offhand, but..." She picked up her phone. "I have her in my email. Girl, I never delete emails."

I laughed.

Nyla bounced her shoulders up and down in triumph. "Here you go. Miranda Blackwell. She's the publicist for quite a few artists and musicians. Her agency, Magnolia Media, is based here in Charleston."

"Thanks for passing that along. I imagine a publicist may know a lot and even have access to Rebecca's calendar." I glanced over at the wave bars on the screen that Nyla B had finished editing for me. "So do you really think the interview is good?"

Nyla smiled at me. "You're nervous?"

"Yes! There are a lot of people covering news about Rebecca. I'm a grain of sand."

Nyla pointed at me. "No, you're a whole sandbox. This is going to get attention. You got an exclusive interview. That's something."

I sighed. "I don't want it to blow up and cause more trouble for Claude. He trusted me with this interview."

Nyla quirked an eyebrow. "It will be fine. When do you plan to release it?"

I blew out a breath. "I'm thinking Monday. I want some other folks to listen to it, including Claude."

A LATTE MAYHEM

Nyla leaned forward like she was about to say something, then she shut her mouth.

"What were you about to say?"

She shook her head. "Nothing. That's really thoughtful of you. Most folks put the story out there to get ratings or likes on social media. You really care about people." She tilted her head with a smile. "By the way, how's the detective boyfriend feeling about all this?"

I grimaced. "He's one of the people I want to listen to the podcast. I'm not trying to sensationalize Rebecca's death. If anything, I want to humanize her in the midst of everybody speculating. Now that you heard Claude's interview, what do you think?"

Nyla finished off the cinnamon roll she'd been enjoying. "Oh, I wasn't one of those who thought Claude had anything to do with Rebecca's death. But there are those who flat out believe he's not innocent, mainly Rebecca's sister. I will say the guy Rebecca was dating should have had as much scrutiny on him as Claude."

I snapped my fingers. "Ethan Turner. I've been researching him."

Nyla nodded. "He was on the show one time too, before he hooked up with Rebecca. He was doing the rounds, talking about his new startup Synaptic. He struck me as a real arrogant type. Pretty boy who grew up filthy rich. His company was just another toy out of many. I was shocked when Rebecca started dating him. I can't think of two people that were more opposite."

"Fay said something similar. I really do appreciate you helping me edit this first episode."

"Not a problem. There is new editing software out there now. AI is making things a lot easier. I will send you a link. The way it works, you wouldn't even have to use this equipment. Just upload your .wav file, let the software transcribe it and you can edit the audio by deleting the text. It's like working with a document."

"That sounds super easy. Yes, please send it to me."

"Will do." Nyla stood. "Okay, girlfriend, I need to call it a night. You let me know when you get this out into the world and I will help promote it on the radio station. You know we love to support local content creators. Any idea who you will interview next?"

I shrugged. "I'm hoping to talk to Rebecca's sister. I've sent her a few emails and left a voicemail. So far she hasn't responded. Thanks for the tip on the publicist. I imagine that could be a good interview too."

We walked out of the studio and I locked the door. I peeked up the stairs and thought about saying something to Claude, but then thought better of it. Though it was early summer, the sun had gone down. He would probably be deep into a canvas. Possibly the one he'd been working on of Rebecca.

Nyla and I walked out into the humid air toward our cars.

"You know the gala is coming up soon." Nyla mentioned. "It's going to be an interesting event now that they've found Rebecca's remains. That mural Rebecca did there was her last major piece of work. Ashford Art Gallery must be getting lots of traffic."

"Yeah, Fay received an invitation. She mentioned trying to get one for me. Do you think it's worth going?"

Nyla grinned. "I've been a few times. Us grownups don't get to dress up much. It's a great time to enjoy the finer things in life. The food is always good. You know the usual cheese and crackers, fruit situation, but there's also huge jumbo shrimp, and even caviar. But that stuff looks nasty to me."

I laughed. "The food and the art sound like a good reason to attend."

Nyla faced me before she opened her car door. "You should go. It's a great event and you'll get to rub elbows with some of the most talented artists in Charleson. Plus, my sister will have an exhibit this year."

"Really? That's awesome! I remember when Simone was taking photos for the yearbook back in high school. Now she's a big-time photographer and you're the hottest DJ in the southeast."

Nyla pointed her finger at me. "You know it. Let me know how it works out. I hope to see you at the gala."

I climbed into my car and watched Nyla drive off in her BMW. I admired my friend and appreciated her even more. She not only helped me mix the first episode but gave me pointers on how to tackle it myself next time. Combined with the information she shared, it was a productive evening.

I needed to officially launch the second season of the *Cold Justice* podcast to the world.

Chapter 5
The Weekend Committee

Friday, June 14, 6:35 p.m.

I'd had just enough time after closing the café to take a quick shower. I was glad I'd shaved my legs on my day off. Opting for a big, loose white shirt that I tied at the waist over denim shorts, I slipped on my sandals just as Andre rang the doorbell.

Our mutual friends, recent newlyweds Leesa and Chris Black, had invited us over. A few weeks before Leesa and Chris tied the knot, they'd started a couples only night on Fridays. Sometimes Leesa's brother, Cedric Patterson and his wife Carmen came over as well. It was a lot of fun. There was music and games, and the night always included a meal, usually grilled burgers, wings or pizza, craft beer for the guys and wine for the ladies.

We hadn't seen Leesa and Chris since their wedding.

"Hey, you two." Leesa gushed as I walked through the door.

"The newlyweds." I hugged Leesa and then Chris. "Where are the kids?"

Leesa and Chris had a three year old son together plus Leesa's oldest daughter Kisha.

"They're over with my mom. She picked them up from daycare and will drop them off in the morning. They miss Aunty Joss."

"I miss them too." I loved being around kids, and on occasion, I babysat Leesa's children. They were both pretty well-behaved. I looked over at Andre. I'd only met a few of Andre's relatives, but I could tell he was a favorite uncle.

A man who loved kids. That made him even sexier in my book.

Chris and Andre headed out to the backyard toward the grill, and I followed Leesa into the kitchen.

Leesa said, "Chris couldn't wait to grill, so we splurged on New York strip steaks tonight. The baked potatoes are in the oven, and I'm chopping up some bacon in case anyone wants them loaded."

I looked around the kitchen. A big pitcher of tea sat on one counter alongside a large bowl of salad. On another, various condiments and salad dressing were on a tray. "Girl, you are so organized. Do you need me to do anything?"

"Nope. Tell me what's going on with you." She winked at me. "You and Andre still hot and heavy?"

I moaned a little and glanced back at the patio door. I could see Chris and Andre laughing about something. "We definitely still have the hots for each other, but we're taking it slow. Maybe too slow."

"That's not a bad thing. You always said you wanted something closer to the real thing. Real is hard to do when the physical stuff gets in the way. Clouds your judgment."

I narrowed my eyes. "Girl, do you know how much you sound like your mother, and mine too."

Leesa pursed her lips. "Well, I am Eugeena Patterson's daughter. Her ways were bound to rub off on me. Seriously, what else have you been up to besides working at the café? Did you give any more thought to starting the podcast again?"

"I'm glad you asked. I'm actually launching season two on Monday."

"Oh, what's the topic?"

"I have an exclusive interview with Claude about Rebecca Montgomery's disappearance."

"What?" Leesa placed her hands on her hips. "Joss, didn't they just find the remains of her body?"

I nodded. "I know. I know. The timing. The subject matter. It might bring more attention to the *Cold Justice* podcast than the first season. I have the interview on my phone, but I would love it if a few more people listened to it. I'm really kind of anxious about it."

"Sure, you should play it at dinner. Does Andre know?"

I gulped. "He knows I'm interested, but I haven't told him that I've completed my first interview yet."

Leesa raised an eyebrow. "I guess he's going to find out. Better let him know before you make it live to the whole world."

That's what I thought too. I just hope he doesn't discourage me.

Chris and Andre came through the door with platters. One platter held grilled vegetables, the other, beautifully cooked steaks. Our friends certainly knew how to put together a feast.

We had been eating for a while before Leesa nudged me. "So are you going to play it for us?"

Andre glanced over at me. "Play what?"

I started to explain, but Leesa beat me to it. "The first episode of the podcast. Season two starts Monday. We're getting a first listen."

Chris cleared his throat. "Wow, that's cool that you are going to continue with the podcast. The first season was really well done."

"Thank you, Chris." I smiled and pulled out my phone. "Alright, so no one else will have this interview. It's exclusive since Claude hasn't done interviews." I pressed play and nervously went back to my salad as my voice and Claude's responses took over the space.

I focused on Andre to gauge his reaction, but he remained quiet, meticulously slicing into his steak. I knew he still had reservations about me discussing Rebecca's case, given his role as a detective on the same case.

I stopped the podcast midway. "Well, that's a taste of it. If you want to hear more, I'm planning to upload it Sunday night."

Leesa beamed. "It sounds good! I think you're going to get a lot of listeners, especially since Claude's never spoken to anyone about Rebecca before." She turned to Andre. "What did you think of the episode so far? I'm sure you have some unique insights being so close to the case."

Andre set down his fork. "It was well-produced, Joss. Did you mix it yourself?"

I cringed. Did Andre know how long I'd been sitting on the interview? "No, I reached out to Nyla B. I kind of remembered my way around the studio, but I needed some expertise. She came by yesterday and gave me some good tips on how I could cut down on the editing and how to mix the audio levels."

Andre nodded. "So what's the plan for the rest of the season? I can't help but worry about you getting too involved in this. It's an ongoing investigation, and I don't want you to put yourself in danger."

Danger. There was that word again.

Claude mentioned something about Rebecca being in danger, but he still didn't really elaborate during the interview. I got the sense that Claude thought something, or someone, had been bothering Rebecca.

What does Andre know?

Instead of asking him what was in my head, I felt a need to defend my choice for the podcast. "I'm taking the same route I did with the first podcast. I want people to tell their stories of Rebecca. Remind the world that she was a vibrant person and a part of the Sugar Creek community."

Leesa put her chin in her hands. "I think it's wonderful. No one else is doing this. Everyone else is digging in trying to do your job, Andre. Not Joss."

Chris nodded. "I can see both sides. As detectives, we want to make sure our investigation is thorough and uncompromised. But sometimes, a fresh perspective can be invaluable."

Andre leaned back in his seat. "I don't want Joss to become a target. If the person responsible for Rebecca's disappearance feels threatened by Joss's digging, who knows what they might do?"

Leesa stood and placed her hands on my shoulders. "No one is going to bother Joss. I'm sure she knows how to take precautions. And she has you looking out for her, too."

Andre couldn't help but smile. "That's true."

Leesa clapped her hands, making me jump. "Alright, who's up for a game of Spades?"

I was grateful for the change of subject and returning the focus to having a fun Friday night. But when my eyes met Andre's, I knew he had more to say. He just didn't want to spoil the fun.

Friday, June 14, 9:57 p.m.

Leesa and Chris walked away with bragging rights from our game of Spades. Andre and I licked our wounds and chipped in on cleanup duty. Leesa cleaned along the way, so most of the dirty dishes were already in the dishwasher.

We said goodnight and headed out. Hanging out with our friends was fun, and I felt good about it. But I could tell there was a bit of tension in the air – mainly between Andre and I. He put on a good face, laughed and enjoyed the evening. But every time he looked my way, I registered concern behind those intense brown eyes.

Andre drove me home, and the silence in the car was deafening. I had a sinking feeling it had to do with my podcast and my decision to step my toes into Rebecca's disappearance. Unable to bear the tension any longer, I turned to face him. "Andre, are you upset with me?"

He sighed, his eyes fixed on the road ahead. "No, Joss. I'm not upset with you. I'm worried."

I bit my lip, trying to quell the rising anxiety in my chest. Andre sometimes shared parts of his investigation. I wondered how much he would let me know and if he thought he could even trust me now. "Worried about what?"

Andre glanced my way. "Who else do you plan on trying to interview?"

I could see where this was going. Andre didn't want me to interview the person responsible for Rebecca's disappearance. I didn't think anyone that I was going to interview was responsible, but I'd been wrong on guessing whodunit from fictional books and movies.

"Nyla gave me the contact information for the publicist who worked with Rebecca. I'd also like to talk to the sister Olivia. Definitely Vivian Ashford, the gallery owner. Oh yeah, and the boyfriend, Ethan Turner."

Andre grimaced and visibly took a deep breath.

"Oh no! Which one of those people do you not want me to talk to? No, wait. Let me guess. The boyfriend? What do you know, Andre?"

He shook his head. "We still don't have any solid leads. And I shouldn't be talking to you about an ongoing investigation."

"I'm not going to say a word to anyone, you know that." I frowned. "But you're opposed to me talking to Ethan. He probably wouldn't give me or the podcast his time. He's a big time tech mogul."

Andre pulled into the driveway of my grandmother's home. "Don't be surprised if he's interested. I hear Ethan keeps his ear pretty close to social media. His reputation and the chatter about his company are everything to him."

He cut off the engine and we sat in the car. I could see lights on in the living room. Sometimes my grandmother stayed up, which was sweet. But it was pretty late, so I hoped she was already in bed. The trio of cats would keep vigil until I stepped through the door.

Out of courtesy, in case I decided to invite Andre in, Louise kept the lights on and stayed out of sight. Out of sight, but I was sure with a listening ear. My grandmother was known for being the nosy neighbor and chaired the neighborhood watch for years.

Andre broke the silence that had settled over us. "I think the detectives responsible for investigating Rebecca's disappearance should have looked into Ethan Turner more thoroughly. Something about him doesn't sit right with me."

"What happened to the original detectives on the case?"

He leaned his head back against the seat. "Detective Everett Hawkins retired. Detective Grayson Beckett is my new partner. Not a bad guy, but he's a twenty year veteran and definitely looking forward to retirement too. He told me he and Hawkins looked into Ethan Turner's relationship with Rebecca. But then they started focusing more on Claude. It didn't help that Turner lawyered up. It's nearly impossible to get anything out of him, and I find that suspicious."

"Being her boyfriend, you would think he would have wanted her found. Do you think he had something to do with Rebecca's disappearance?"

Andre's jaw clenched. "I don't know for sure, but my gut tells me he knows more than he's letting on. And there's something else..."

I sat up straighter, my heart pounding in my chest. "What is it?"

"Based on the evidence we've gathered so far, I don't think Rebecca was killed in those woods where her body was found. I think she was killed somewhere else, and her body was moved there after the fact."

I felt a chill run down my spine at the thought of someone carrying Rebecca's lifeless body through the woods, disposing of her like she was nothing. It made me feel sick to my stomach.

"That's horrible and creepy. That crime scene would have been cleaned up by now."

He nodded. "Yeah. Whoever did this had time to plan it out and cover their tracks. I don't know if it was random or if Rebecca knew her killer, but we're going with the latter."

I swallowed hard, trying to process the weight of his words. "So you're not going to bother Claude?"

Andre's eyes softened. "I know you interviewed him first because you're worried about him. Olivia Montgomery, the vic's sister, is bent on putting the heat on Claude, but there's no evidence. Beckett admitted him and his old partner probably spent too long concentrating on Claude."

"I wish they would apologize to him. You know one of those crazy social media folks snuck into the Lofts to bother Claude. He doesn't need that kind of harassment."

Andre frowned. "No, he doesn't. Tell Claude the next time that happens, he should press charges for trespassing. He can call me."

"I will. So now what? Are you okay with me reaching out to the other people? Besides Ethan Turner, of course."

He reached for my hand. "I know how much you've been wanting to get back into podcasting. I don't need to tell you to be careful with your questions. You don't want to be slammed with slander charges."

I squeezed his hand back, enjoying the warmth of his hands wrapped around mine. "I certainly don't want that kind of attention."

"Good." He brought my hand to his lips and pressed a soft kiss to my knuckles. Then he leaned over. "I'd like a proper good night kiss."

He didn't have to ask me twice.

A LATTE MAYHEM

Sunday, June 16, 2:14 p.m.

I worked at the café on Saturday. Tourist season had begun and it was nonstop action. When Sunday morning arrived, I wanted to stay under the covers, but I'd promised my great aunts I would go to church with them. They'd convinced my mother to show up as well. Both of us had been heathens for a few Sundays in a row.

Aunt Ruth and Aunt Thelma were my grandfather's youngest sisters. They'd kept his untimely death in the spotlight in the community for many years before they grew too old to continue the fight. When Mom discovered them during her search for her biological parents, both sisters embraced us – the missing part of their brother's long lost family.

I grew up with a small family. My dad, mom and brother. Dad didn't have a large family himself, having lost his mom when he was younger and never knowing his dad. My mom's adoptive parents had also passed, the result of one terminal illness after the next. That loss drove her search for more family and ultimately, to her discovering she'd been adopted.

Since my dad's death, my brother had disappeared. Well, I wouldn't call it a typical missing person's case. He had a social media presence and occasionally dropped a post about whatever he was doing in the world. Usually it was a party or gathering with people I didn't know. I couldn't tell if he had a significant other, but there were always women. He called Mom on Mother's Day last month. Out of the blue, on my birthday or Christmas, I might get a text from him.

Family was pretty important to me. But those relationships seemed so fragile sometimes as things changed in the blink of an eye.

After church, we rode back to my aunts' home for Sunday dinner. Despite the summer weather, my great aunts loved being in the kitchen. Aunt Ruth, the oldest sister, made the main dish, one of my favorites, Chicken Bog. The Lowcountry dish included chicken, sausage and rice. We ate and laughed during dinner. It was refreshing to see my mom relaxed. Our relationship was strained, but the aunties were able to get her to be herself. By the time Aunt Thelma brought out her specialty, 7-up pound cake, which was so good and moist, the conversation switched to more serious concerns.

Aunt Thelma asked, "So, Joss, are you doing okay? You've been kind of quiet today."

Aunt Ruth teased. "She's probably thinking about that man of hers. You need to bring him back by here so we can cook for him."

I grinned. "He's headed up to Charlotte this weekend to see his family. One of his sisters will be having a baby soon."

My mom nodded. "Sounds like he's a good son and brother. I'm sure his job keeps him pretty busy."

"Yeah. I haven't met all of his sisters yet. When his mother and older sister came to visit, they were pretty nice. I can't believe he has like three sisters."

Aunt Ruth cackled. "That makes him a great student of women."

I had to admit that part of Andre was very appealing. But also scary. After meeting his mom and older sister during a brief affair on Easter weekend, I couldn't imagine being around his mom and all three sisters. Andre warned me that his younger two sisters were super protective.

Ready to move on from the topic of my boyfriend, I'd been waiting for an opening all afternoon. And this was probably as good as it would get. "So, I'm bringing back the podcast."

All three women looked at me. My mom spoke first. She'd been against me sharing about her father's murder to the 'whole wide world' as she put it. But she eventually came around.

She gave me that look that made me cringe inside. "What's the podcast about this time?"

"Well, you know my friend Claude?"

Aunt Ruth interrupted. "The one who painted the portrait of August?"

"That's him. He had a friend disappear about three years ago. I'm sure you've heard about her remains being discovered if you've watched the news."

Aunt Thelma sucked in a breath. "Oh Lord, yes. Ruth, we saw that on the television last night. She was an artist too."

Aunt Ruth nodded. "Painted those colorful murals on the side of buildings."

"Yes. Rebecca Montgomery."

My mother stared at me. "What exactly are you going to be talking about on the podcast? This young woman was obviously killed. That's for the police to investigate. I'm sure Andre told you that." She knitted her eyebrows together, almost making a unibrow. "Or does he not know what you're up to? Child, you better not go messing up—"

"Whoa, whoa, Mom. He knows. And of course I'm not trying to be a cop here. It will be like the podcast I did for Granddad. Give people an opportunity to talk about Rebecca, remind others of who she was to the community. She's more than what some hiker and their dog found in the woods."

Aunt Ruth patted my hand. "That sounds good, baby."

Aunt Thelma agreed. "We enjoyed being interviewed on your podcast. No one ever let us talk about our brother like that before."

My mom frowned. "This is different. This Rebecca woman, was she close to your age?"

I shook my head. "She was a bit older. Around Fay's age, late thirties. Look, I don't want you all to worry. I wanted to let you know what I was up to. Right now I only have one interview. It may be hard to get other people to talk to me. We'll see what happens when the podcast comes out tomorrow morning."

Aunt Ruth and Aunt Thelma seemed satisfied with my answer. Mom and I cleaned off the table and shooed them both outside to sit on the patio. The rule was since they did all the cooking, we would clean up the kitchen.

I busied myself by filling the sink full of soapy water. My great aunts were pretty old-fashioned and didn't have a dishwasher. While I washed dishes, my mom piled the plates and pans next to me. She didn't say anything, but I could feel the tension emanating from her as she switched over to rubbing dishes dry. I wanted to tease her, ask her if she planned on rubbing the design off the plates but thought better of it. I might be grown, but I wasn't that grown to tick my mom off unnecessarily.

Although I think I managed to do that anyway.

With the last of the utensils washed, I dried my hands and waited. I knew it was coming.

My mom started talking as though we hadn't been silent for the last twenty minutes. "Joss, you know I worry about you. You've always had this way of getting into things. It's bad enough your brother has turned my hair gray with his shenanigans. I need one of you to be normal."

I remembered not to roll my eyes. "I'm here, Mom, having Sunday afternoon dinner with you and the aunties. I've been a good girl, even getting up on time to go to church. My bills are all up-to-date and I'm working hard at the café. I even have a boyfriend, who by the way has me practicing celibacy. Who knows, he could be the one."

My mom stopped pacing and quirked her eyebrow. "Not that I'm in your business like that, but you really haven't done ... you know ... with that man."

"Like I said, I've been a good girl. You should be proud."

"I am proud of you, baby." My mom smiled. "You really think he could be the one?"

I grinned. "I hope so. I mean so far he's still putting up with me."

I had a lot riding on how I handled season two of this podcast. I would do my best to heed Andre's warnings.

Chapter 6
Buzz Kill

COLD JUSTICE PODCAST

Season 2, Episode 1: A Close Friend
Published: June 17

Joss: Welcome to the Season Two of the *Cold Justice* podcast. I'm your host, Joss Miller. It's been awhile since launching the first season last fall. I want to thank all my listeners for supporting me as I shared the almost forgotten case around my grandfather's murder. Your feedback and encouragement has motivated me to continue to tell stories of people in our community.

People we shouldn't forget.

This season we're diving into the mysterious disappearance of the brilliant artist and activist, Rebecca Montgomery. This past week the Charleston Police Department set up a press conference. I'm going to play a small sound bite from Police Chief Nolan Whitaker.

"Our medical examiner has identified the body found in Francis Marion State Forest as that of Rebecca Montgomery. We suspect foul play and will be investigating this case to find out what happened to her. If there is anyone who knows something, we urge you to come forward and talk to us. The tip line is open as well."

Joss: With these recent developments, I reached out to a fellow artist and good friend of mine, Claude McKnight. I felt like it was important for the first episode of this season to be with Claude, who was also a close friend of the late Rebecca Montgomery. He has agreed to speak with me and share his side of the story.

Let me get this out of the way. I'm not here to vilify anyone for ratings or likes. I want this podcast to be a vehicle for sharing about a person whose life was cruelly snatched away and the effect that loss has had on the people who knew her.

As background for this interview, the days leading up to Rebecca's disappearance three years ago became a horrific time for Claude. Rebecca's sister, Olivia, reported seeing Claude and Rebecca engaged in a heated argument the day before she went missing. This revelation cast aspersion over Claude, keeping him under the scrutiny of the police.

I want to repeat that the police did not find Claude guilty of any wrongdoing. Claude will share details about his last interactions with Rebecca and shed some light on her state of mind.

This is the *Cold Justice* podcast. Let's get into it!

Joss: Claude, thank you for agreeing to speak with me today. I know this hasn't been an easy road for you, but I believe your perspective is crucial to understanding what happened to Rebecca. Let's start from the beginning. Can you tell me about your friendship with Rebecca and how it all began?

Claude: Thanks for having me, Joss (takes a deep breath). Rebecca and I go way back. I've known Becca, that's what I called her, all my life. We went to school together, took the same art classes, we even... went to the senior prom together.

Joss: High school sweethearts?

Claude: No, nothing like that. Becca was special to me. Always stuck up for me when we were growing up. The only time we weren't in touch was when she went to Savannah. When she was back in town, it was like old times.

Joss: I know several years have passed. But, can you remember the last time you saw or spoke to Rebecca?

Claude: A few days after the gala.

Joss: You're referring to the annual gala at the Ashford Art Gallery?

Claude: Yes. I had heard about the gala, but never attended. I went that year to support Becca. That night she should have been celebrating what she'd created. But she seemed...disturbed, like something was bugging her. I asked her what was bothering her, but she brushed it off. Truthfully, she seemed off long before that night. The night of the gala she seemed... scared.

Joss: Scared? And you had no inkling about what was bothering her?

Claude: No. I tried to press further. Let her know I could help, but she kept saying no one could help her. Becca seemed frustrated and distant, so I left. Her sister took it as an argument. But I could feel the fear radiating off Becca.

Joss: You thought she was in danger. Did Rebecca have any complex relationships that you're aware of?

Claude: (quiet for a few seconds) I thought she did, but I don't want to speculate as others seem to like to do about me. I will say she had some people around her that didn't value her as a person.

Becca was a private person, especially when it came to her personal life. Sometimes it's hard to ask for help. I'm the same way, so I could relate. Sometimes you want to be in your own thoughts and think about what's next.

After I left the gala, I figured she would talk to me or another mutual friend when she was ready. Apparently, she never had the chance. Her sister showed up at my place yelling that Becca was missing like I did something. The crazy thing was I wasn't the last person who saw her alive (huff). That's all I'm going to say.

Joss: I'm so sorry for your loss, Claude. Before we finish, is there anything else you want to share about Rebecca?

Claude: Only that she was one of the most gifted artists I've ever known. She cared about her work, and she cared about her community. She didn't deserve whatever happened to her.

I hope whoever is responsible will be found and brought to justice.

Monday, June 17, 6:54 a.m.

I woke earlier than usual and arrived at the café early to help Fay open. She was in the back pulling her famous mini sweet potato pies out of the oven. She looked up at me with a smile as I passed her. "Hey, you're here earlier than usual."

I placed my bag in my locker and grabbed my Sugar Creek café apron. As I wrapped it around me, my words tumbled out. "I couldn't sleep. I really did it! The first podcast of season two is out in the world."

Fay grinned. "I heard it. Good job getting Claude to tell his side of the story."

My jaw dropped. "Wait, you heard it already? I made it live last night, like after midnight."

Fay nodded. "I subscribed to your podcast last fall. I saw the notification on my phone this morning when I woke up. I listened to it as I baked."

A LATTE MAYHEM

"Wow. I wonder how many people heard it. I got mixed feedback from family and friends over the weekend, and I have no idea if I can pull off a full season. So many people are talking about what happened to Rebecca, suppose my little ole' podcast gets lost in a sea of investigative reporting."

Fay pointed to me. "You need to take a breath. I don't think you realize fully what you pulled off. You have an exclusive interview with Claude McKnight, one of Becca's closest friends. I wouldn't be surprised if you start hearing from more people. You will have to be selective."

"I can only hope. I do have a list of people I've reached out to. I'll see who bites first." I steepled my hands together under my chin. "Do you really think people will listen to Claude's side of the story? I thought he handled himself well, although some of the questions were emotional for him."

Fay finished sliding a spatula under the mini pies to lift them off the pan and onto a tray. She picked up the tray. "Can you grab that tray of cinnamon rolls?"

"Sure thing." I followed behind Fay. My mouth watered from the smell of the cinnamon.

While placing the pastries inside the protective glass shelves, Fay said. "Joss, you have such a human touch about you. People will see that you care and have pure intentions. Plus, Claude trusted you."

I fretted. "I hope he doesn't have any regrets. I should check on him later today." I looked up, noticing movement around the cafe window. " Are you ready to open? I can already see folks outside the door."

Fay blew out a breath. "Let's do this."

By the time eight o'clock came, I soon found out Fay wasn't the only person who'd heard the episode. Sugar Creek was a small community. A lot of people who came into the café were repeat customers. I almost felt like a celebrity with all the comments. I hoped people would treat Claude as warmly. My friend needed a break.

Eleanor came rushing in later than usual. She approached the counter beaming. "You did a great job. I'm so proud of you."

"Thanks! I'm glad Claude felt comfortable about sharing his friendship with Rebecca. I'm not sure if he's heard the podcast yet."

The smile dropped from her face. "He may not listen to it. Claude reminds me of his father. They liked to do things and then move on. But I'm pretty sure it was cathartic for him to talk to you."

"I hope so. What will you have this morning?"

Eleanor rubbed her hands together. "One of those cinnamon rolls with a vanilla latte, please."

"Awesome! I will bring it over to you."

Another hour passed and we sold out of the cinnamon rolls. After wiping down tables, I noticed the canisters of sugar packets and creamers were low and headed to the back for more condiments. I was replenishing the supply when the café door chimed. It'd been slow for at least twenty minutes.

I circled the corner of the condiment counter. Liam Holbrook was peering up at the menu.

He caught sight of me and started grinning.

I didn't trust the grin. I also didn't know why he was looking at the menu when he bought the same thing all the time.

"A barista and a journalist?"

I stared at him, annoyed that he'd come into the café. I guess I was still riled from his attempt to invade Claude's space. "These days journalist come in all shapes and sizes."

Liam grinned. "Of course. I have a Mass Communications degree from the College of Charleston. And I've won awards for my investigative journalism."

I gave him a blank look.

Was I supposed to care?

I also wanted to ask what kind of awards. I'd seen Liam's social media posts and they were not award worthy. More like clickbait. I had to remind myself he was a customer, so I pasted on a smile even though I didn't feel like it. "What can I get you this morning?"

"A large black coffee for me." He leaned on the counter as I went over to pull a cup. "It's Joss, right? I heard your interview with Claude. Impressive stuff. What do you say we collaborate on future interviews? I've got some juicy leads and a larger following that could really boost your ratings."

I placed the steaming cup on the counter in front of him. "Would you like anything else with the coffee?"

Liam looked annoyed that I'd ignored his proposition. "No, but did you hear what I said?"

I rang up his coffee. "That will be $2.50."

He blew out a breath and swiped his card. "I have very good sponsors. I didn't notice if your podcast had any sponsors."

I didn't but I wasn't doing the *Cold Justice* podcast for the money. At least not yet. I knew the content creators economy was fierce about being the next big influencer and making money for sponsorships. Somehow, that didn't feel right to me.

My cheeks were throbbing as I attempted to smile again. "Thanks, but I'm not ready for all that hassle and I prefer to work alone."

Liam shrugged. "Suit yourself, but you're missing out on a golden opportunity. I can help you get way more money than what you get working behind this counter."

If he thought he was insulting me, he was wrong.

I loved being a barista. And with all his following in the world, he still couldn't get an interview with Claude. But I wasn't about to rub that in his face. I could tell it bothered him.

"Have a good day. Happy investigating!" I said with a real smile.

He looked at me and offered a quick salute before turning away.

As he walked away, Fay came up behind me. "Was he bothering you?"

I sighed. "I think he was a little upset that I got the interview with Claude. Did you know he trespassed by tricking Claude into letting him into the Lofts?"

Fay turned up her nose. "I told you he's the worst. He better be glad he buys coffee regularly." Her face suddenly lit up, and she reached into her apron pocket and pulled out an elegant envelope. "Hey, I managed to get you an invitation to the upcoming gala."

My eyes widened in surprise and gratitude. "Fay, that's amazing! Thank you so much."

Fay winked. "Like I said, you should get your man to dress up in a tux and come with you."

"I will see what he says when I ask him."

"I haven't seen him around the café in a few days. I hope I didn't scare him off last week."

I shook my head. "No, the case is keeping him busy."

Fay's smile drooped and her voice lowered. "Is he working on ... Becca's case?"

"Yes. And you can be assured that he's determined to find out what happened to her. And don't worry, he listened to the episode before I published it."

Fay raised an eyebrow. "That's good that you got his blessing."

I wasn't exactly sure if that was the case, but I understood Andre's concerns. As I forged ahead with the next episode, I hoped our relationship wouldn't be affected. That was the last thing I wanted to happen.

A LATTE MAYHEM

Monday, June 17, 1:34 p.m.

With the summer months and tourist season, things picked up before the lunch crowd and we hustled behind the counter getting orders ready. When things finally slowed, I grabbed a flaky croissant filled with chicken salad mixed with cranberries and pecans piled on fresh greens and an iced vanilla latte and headed over to a table near Eleanor. The tap of keys sounded beside me as I ate. Since Eleanor was on a roll today, I decided not to disturb her. I pulled out my phone and saw I had a text from Andre.

> **Andre:** Hey, just checking in. I miss stopping by the café. This coffee here at the station isn't hitting it at all.

I smiled and responded.

> **Joss:** I miss seeing you. I've been getting good feedback about the first episode.

The annoying ellipses seemed to go on for a few seconds like Andre had been typing a message. But no message came. Only a thumbs up next to my text.

I wrinkled my nose at his response.

That wasn't satisfying.

I was sure he was busy and I was grateful he reached out during the day. I knew how Andre felt about me doing the podcast, but I still wanted a little more support from him.

So engrossed in the text, I missed Eleanor saying something to me.

When she started waving her hands to get my attention, I turned. "Sorry, Eleanor, were you saying something?"

She smiled. "I know you're glad to get off your feet. Why don't you come over here and sit? We can catch up on how things are going for you."

"Oh, thanks. I heard you typing away over there."

Eleanor shrugged. "I lost steam, which means I need a break."

"Okay. " I picked up my tray and moved into the seat across from Eleanor.

"I heard your run-in with Liam Holbrook earlier," Eleanor said. "You did the right thing by refusing his offer. That man is nothing but trouble."

I sipped my iced latte. "I'm sure he was peeved that I got the interview with Claude."

Eleanor chuckled. "Claude told me yesterday that the reporter had schemed his way inside the Lofts. Unfortunately, there may have been others if Claude hadn't decided to talk to you first."

I swallowed the big bite of chicken salad I'd just taken. "You don't think he will regret talking to me."

Eleanor shook her head. "I invited him over for brunch yesterday afternoon. It's been awhile since he's come over and he seemed in good spirits, especially with everything going on. I think he's also trying to keep from thinking about the fact that they found Rebecca's remains. It's awful, Joss. I really wonder what happened to her."

"I do too." I grimaced. "I also promised Andre I wouldn't dig too hard either. But I want to talk to more people who knew Rebecca. Any ideas?"

"Who's on your list?" Eleanor asked.

I started counting off on my fingers. "Rebecca's sister, Olivia. My friend DJ Nyla B told me about Rebecca's publicist. The gallery owner, Vivian Ashford. There is only one person I know I should interview, but my boyfriend detective warned me away from him."

Eleanor cocked her head at me. "Who? And why?"

I probably shouldn't have said anything. I was certain Andre had trusted me with that information to keep me from talking to Ethan. I looked around. Despite the café being pretty quiet, with only a few customers, I lowered my voice. "What do you know about Ethan Turner?"

"Oh," Eleanor stated. "I've looked into him, but I haven't met or talked with him personally. He's one of the people who refused my inquiry. I reached out to him over a year ago. The police were looking at him as well as Claude. Apparently, Ethan had an argument with Rebecca the night of her mural premiere. A lot of people witnessed it, but that happened three days before her disappearance and the last person she was seen with was Claude..."

I nodded. "Claude received the brunt of the questioning. But technically, he wasn't the last person to see Rebecca."

Eleanor's mouth formed a perfect letter O. "That's right. Her sister showed up after Claude left. But she's been devoted to finding out what happened to her sister."

"I know, but she hasn't helped by blowing up the exchange between Claude and Rebecca. Has the sister ever mentioned anything about Ethan? I know Claude doesn't like him."

Eleanor sighed. "I will say that in my book, which you know is based loosely on Rebecca's disappearance, I leaned more toward the boyfriend. I'm not going to say he did it." She winked. "You will have to read it for yourself when it comes out in the fall."

I grinned. "I look forward to reading it. I was wondering which direction you were going, now that she's been found in real life."

Eleanor's face sobered. "It's unlikely that she would have been alive after all this time. Don't get me wrong, there are real life examples of people getting kidnapped and held at some location for months. Even years. But a lot of those stories end with the victim's death."

I wondered if Rebecca met up with somebody that night or was she forcefully snatched somewhere. She'd gone somewhere. Her keys and pocketbook were missing.

Eleanor interrupted my thoughts. "Rebecca's sister would be a no for me. Olivia has not wanted to talk to me. She's treated me like a reporter rather than an award-winning published author. But I can help you with two of the people you want to interview."

"So you know Miranda Blackwell, Rebecca's publicist?"

Eleanor smiled. "I know Miranda. Her agency helped me schedule my last book tour and they manage my website. Miranda started her public relations firm about ten years ago. She's a fan of my books, which is why I stick with her for marketing. Actually, Rebecca and I were her first clients." Eleanor looked away for a moment, staring absently out the window.

She turned to face me. "I hate to spread rumors, especially when a woman is dead."

I had finished eating and was probably five minutes past my break being over. So, I glanced around the café. I could stretch my break another minute or two. Eleanor had snatched my attention, and I wasn't letting this moment go.

"What are you holding out on telling me?"

Eleanor pulled a napkin into her hand and began twisting it into some origami like creation. "I heard Rebecca had a falling out with Miranda. She didn't want to be represented by the agency anymore."

This seemed to be a trend. People arguing or not getting along with Rebecca.

I frowned. "Was Rebecca Montgomery a difficult person?"

Eleanor shook her head vigorously. "No. I don't think so. I remember when she used to frequent the café. She always spoke to me and was so upbeat. But everyone has a public face and a private one. Plus, she was an artist. We know our Claude can be moody sometimes."

I nodded. "Yeah, but Claude argued with Rebecca because he thought she was hiding something. Like maybe she'd gotten involved in something that frightened her. He described her as being upset but she didn't want him involved."

Eleanor laced her fingers together. "That is curious. Whatever she knew or saw could have been why she was killed."

"That's what I'm thinking. So who was close to Rebecca? Who might she have confided in? She didn't confess anything to Fay or Claude. I've heard her sister say in an interview that they weren't close."

"I do know Vivian Ashford was really fond of her. She commissioned Rebecca to do that art mural at the gallery. Rebecca never did anything small. She loved having a big open wall for her canvas."

I arched an eyebrow. "How do you know Vivian Ashford?"

Eleanor chuckled. "Vivian? She and I go way back, and she has her finger on the pulse of everything that happens in the art community, including the literary side. She has a rather elaborate library in her house which includes books by yours truly."

I sat back. "Wow, you know everyone, Eleanor."

Eleanor stretched her arms out wide. "I'm way past my prime, Joss. I've seen a lot and know a lot about Sugar Creek."

I smiled. "I'm not surprised. I've read your books too. Your fictional town Cypress Landing sounds very familiar."

Eleanor's eyes twinkled. "That's good. Part of the appeal of writing cozy mysteries is the town. It's like another character."

Eleanor tapped her fingers on the booth's table. "I have an idea. I bet Vivian would be delighted to talk to you. She doesn't mind sharing her opinions."

My eyes widened at the opportunity. "Are you sure? She would bring a lot of cred to the podcast."

Eleanor nodded. "I agree. Even though she's been in Charleston almost twenty years, she still has her distinguished British accent. I think you and your listeners would get a kick out of the interview. She's a delightful woman to talk to." Eleanor leaned in. "How do you feel about tea?"

I laughed. "I prefer coffee, but a decent cup of tea is good. Why?"

Eleanor clasped her hands together. "Vivian has… I guess you can call it a tea party on the fourth Sunday of every month at the gallery. I can introduce you to her."

"That would be awesome." I said, already mentally composing my interview questions. "The gala is coming up in early July. Are you going?"

Eleanor hugged herself. "Oh yes. That is the event of the summer. It's always after the Fourth of July, but there are just as many fireworks, figuratively speaking. It's more of an extravagant show of art and the wealthy people who can buy it. This old gal doesn't get to dress up often, so I always make sure to spend money on a nice formal dress."

"Oh, wow. It's formal." I thought about what I had in my closet. I'd been budgeting for a new car since repairs were starting to get pricey for my Honda Civic.

"Do you know how Ethan Turner's company Synaptic became the sponsor of the gala? It seems like an odd fit for a tech company."

Eleanor shook her head. "Not necessarily. But Vivian is business savvy. She may have inherited the gallery from her late husband, but trust me, she's the one who made it into the powerhouse it is today. I believe she thinks of Ethan like a son. She sits on the Synaptic board too."

I heard the bell chimes of the door opening. "Oh, I need to get back. I took a much longer break than I should have. Thanks, Eleanor. It was good talking to you. I think I have clearer direction for the next podcast episode. Sounds like I should focus on the publicist first."

Eleanor nodded. "I agree. Do you need her contact information?"

I slid out of the booth and grabbed my tray. "Actually, I have it from Nyla. But are you okay if I also use your name as a reference?"

"Absolutely. Let me know how it goes." Eleanor waved as I walked away.

With Eleanor's insights and the possibility of introductions, I felt like I could move ahead with the remainder of the podcast season.

I just needed to convince people to talk to me.

Chapter 7
No Bad Publicity

Wednesday, June 19, 9:56 a.m.

Sometimes it's definitely who you know. Eleanor and Nyla B's names came through for me. I touched base with Miranda Blackwell and she invited me to her office. She didn't confirm that she wanted to do an interview, but she did mention she was open to a conversation. I had a feeling she wanted to meet me in person to see what I was about. That was cool with me. So despite Wednesdays being my day off, it would be a busy one for me. I rose earlier to write up my questions. I wanted to be prepared, just in case.

Thanks to Nyla B's tips, I had a solid plan for recording and editing future interviews. Interestingly, the software she suggested was a Synaptic product. I downloaded the app to my phone so I could record the interview.

I tested it a few times and loved how the software transcribed my recordings and could sync to my MacBook. I edited the recording by adjusting the transcript. At first, I balked at the monthly subscription. But figured it would be worth it to use for a few months. The audio sounded much more professional.

For a brief moment, the conversation I had with Liam earlier this week came to mind. While there was no way I wanted to work with the man, he did prompt ideas of sponsorship and how I could generate some income to take care of these extra expenses. I would trust God to guide me. I felt good that things were moving in the right direction and that the timing was perfect. I was so pumped that before I left, I organized my files from the first season and started a folder for the new season.

Season Two > Episode Two: Miranda Blackwell

On my way downstairs, I called to my grandmother, but I didn't hear her. She'd definitely been up. The coffee was still piping hot in the thermal coffeemaker I'd gifted her this past Christmas. I grabbed a mug of coffee and spread some cream cheese on a blueberry bagel.

The bagels came from a new bakery that opened up earlier this year in a more populated part of town. Interestingly, they served coffee too. I'd mentioned them to Fay, but the competition didn't bother her. She was more concerned about Rick

Nelson still trying to push his development project to the city council. I loved the location of the café and I know Fay did too, which was why she refused to sell.

When I walked out on the porch, I found my grandmother in the yard. She was with our next door neighbors, Eugeena Patterson-Jones and her husband, Amos Jones. I couldn't walk past them without saying hello. I glanced down at my phone, I had just enough time to greet my favorite neighbors.

I walked up and Amos smiled, lifting his ball cap off his head in greeting. He sat on top of a riding lawn mower. Thankfully, Amos kept my grandmother's yard in good shape whenever he did the Jones' landscaping.

"Ms. Joss, how are you doing this morning?" Eugeena opened her arms.

Always welcoming a hug, I walked right into her arms for a good squeeze. "I'm good." I looked over at my grandmother who was grinning. "I was wondering where you were. Any good gossip I should know about?"

The three older folks laughed as if they all shared an inside joke.

My grandmother placed her hands on my shoulder. "I was just telling them that you started the podcast again."

Eugeena shook her head. "Louise is proud of you. I haven't heard the first interview yet, but Leesa told me it was good. You all got together on Friday with each other. How's that young man of yours doing?"

I blushed. "Andre is good." I said that but I wasn't really sure. I'd called him last night, but he sounded so tired, we barely stayed on the phone ten minutes. I let him know I was talking to Miranda Blackwell and casually asked him if he knew Rebecca had a falling out with her publicist. I wasn't sure if he was too tired to hear me or if he was stuck on Ethan Turner. I had a feeling it was the latter.

My grandmother asked, "Where are you heading?"

"I'm going to talk to Miranda Blackwell. She was Rebecca Montgomery's publicist."

Amos asked, "That's an interesting choice for an interview. What do you hope to find out?"

Amos was a retired homicide detective. Between him and his wife Eugeena, they liked to do some investigations of their own. So I felt pretty good with sharing my idea with them. "Rebecca had been with her publicist since the beginning of her career. When you listen to the interview I did with Rebecca's close friend Claude McKnight, he mentions that something was going on with her. I learned yesterday that Rebecca suddenly wanted to cut ties with Miranda. Seems strange after all the years that she'd handled Rebecca's PR."

Eugeena crossed her arms like a schoolteacher. "You're going to be careful not to ask her anything that will make her defensive, right?"

"Oh, of course not. I want her to talk to me about their professional relationship and friendship. I'm taking the same angle I did with my first podcast. I don't want the people I interview to think I'm interrogating them."

Eugeena nodded. "Let them feel free to talk to you."

"You will probably get a lot from them when they talk freely." Amos agreed. He raised a thick, gray eyebrow at me. "I'm sure Detective Baez has warned you to be careful."

I nodded. "All of you cops, including the retired ones, all think the same."

Amos chuckled. "It pays to be cautious. Cops see all the bad sides of people."

My grandmother rubbed my back. "I love your mission, Joss. I'm so proud of you."

"Thank you. And I appreciate you both, Ms. Eugeena and Mr. Amos. I need to run so I can get downtown. It's going to be hard finding a parking space."

I climbed into my blazing hot car, making sure the AC vents blasted my face. I didn't put on that much makeup, but I also didn't want to look like a hot sweaty mess. Despite all the encouragement I'd received, butterflies fluttered in my stomach and my hands shook a bit as I gripped the steering wheel. I had no idea if Miranda would consent to an interview. What was that old saying? There's no such thing as bad publicity.

But what if Miranda knew what troubled Rebecca? Did Rebecca's death also haunt Miranda too?

Wednesday, June 19, 11:00 a.m.

I hadn't looked at the weather forecast for the day, but I sensed it was going to rain. It was hot enough for a good, late-afternoon summer thunderstorm. Traffic grew more congested as I drew closer to the historic area around Meeting Street.

When I talked to Miranda Blackwell briefly on the phone yesterday, she seemed friendly enough. But she misunderstood my request at first.

The woman had gushed. "Oh, we've worked with podcasters before. We would love to work with you on a marketing plan."

"Uhm, that sounds cool," I'd replied. "But I was hoping to possibly interview you about Rebecca Montgomery, your former client."

"Oh... Of course." Miranda's voice had faltered. "I can't believe they found her after all this time."

I thought she might have politely hung up on me.

"Hello, are you still there?" I fully expected to hear a dial tone or a firm no.

"Yes, we should talk. I have an opening at eleven o'clock in the morning. But first, I'd like to hear more about your podcast."

Noticing that I had a quarter tank of gas, I really hoped this wasn't going to be a waste of time. Magnolia Media was located on East Bay Street which faced the waterfront. Salty fragrances from the nearby Atlantic Ocean permeated my car as I sought out a convenient parking garage. I knew finding street parking wouldn't be feasible. I swerved inside a parking garage and plucked a white ticket from the machine. A few minutes later, I pulled into a parking space.

With about seven minutes to spare, I made my way to an elevator that would take me street level. I stepped out, embracing the slight breeze that wafted from the water. Good thing I pulled my hair up into an afro puff. I loved wearing big hair, but the humidity this time of year was not my friend.

Charleston wasn't like typical cities with high rises. The buildings boasted centuries of architecture and along East Bay street were cobblestone sidewalks. Thankfully, I remembered to wear flats as I weaved in between tourists toward my destination. Once inside, I shook my yellow blouse away from my skin, grateful for the chilly air-conditioned air inside the lobby. I headed over to a floor plan on a wall. My destination, Magnolia Media, was on the second floor. I glanced at the stairs. Most of these older businesses didn't have elevators.

I couldn't complain about not getting exercise today. At the top of the mahogany staircase, the sleek, modern lobby of Magnolia Media greeted me. A large gold magnolia leaf and the company's name in modern block lettering hung above the receptionist's desk. I pasted on a smile and walked up to a full-figured woman in an emerald-green blouse. She reminded me a little of the singer Adele before her weight loss.

"Hi, welcome to Magnolia Media. How can I help you?"

I read the gold-plated nameplate on the desk.

Angie Blackwell.

Is she related to Miranda? That would make this a family business.

A LATTE MAYHEM

"Hey, my name is Joss Miller. I have an appointment."

Angie smiled and turned to her computer monitor. After tapping a few keys, she said. "Yes, there you are. Miranda will be with you in a few minutes. She's with a client right now."

I nodded. "I noticed your last name is Blackwell too. Are you related to Miranda?"

Angie grimaced. "Yes. I'm the youngest sister. There are four of us, all sisters. Miranda is the oldest." She pulled out a brochure. "You're welcome to read more about our services. Magnolia Media has some great clients."

I reached for the brochure. "I look forward to learning more."

The chairs in the seating area were plush and rather comfortable. I settled in and leafed through the brochure. Magnolia Media boasted some major clients. They even included a quote from Eleanor and a picture of her signing one of her books. I flipped the page and stared at the photo of Rebecca that had been on display everywhere. Under the photograph, the caption read:

PHOTO CREDIT: MAGNOLIA MEDIA

Rebecca had to have been a big client. They still kept her as a part of their advertisement after all this time, or maybe this was an old brochure.

I heard a door open and glanced up to see a tall man enter the hallway. There was something familiar about his chiseled jawline. The man wore his dark hair long at the top so that it swung to one side.

Wait, isn't that...

Ethan Turner. I'd Googled plenty of images of him the past few days. Though I'd never met him in person, he was easily recognizable. From where I sat perched on the waiting room chair, I could tell the photos I'd seen of him didn't do him justice. As I stared, he swept the hair back from his face only for it to glide back in place.

A woman stepped out and placed her hand on his chest. Her blond tresses were pulled back into a smooth ponytail. Ethan leaned down and kissed the woman whom I assumed was Miranda Blackwell.

That kiss was not for a client.

"Don't worry. Everything will be okay."

I'd never heard Ethan's voice. It wasn't very deep, but still manly and commanding.

The woman crossed her arms. "It's been hard. We can't get this kind of attention on a good day. Now the media won't leave us alone."

I gulped and felt a bit of unease. Maybe I shouldn't have come.

Was this a mistake?

My doubts had my mind so jumbled I hadn't realized Ethan was walking toward me.

He didn't respond to Angie despite her saying, "Have a good day, Ethan."

I glanced at her face after Ethan swept by her. It could have been my projection, but she looked disappointed that he hadn't acknowledged her.

He had to walk by me to get to the stairs so I stared. He was indeed blessed with good looks. Was that what captured Rebecca's attention? Did she fall for the way his eyes bore into you? I sucked in a breath.

Oh, wait. He's actually looking at me.

The way his blue eyes roamed over me, I wished I hadn't made eye contact. I looked away, praying he didn't think I was flirting. A man that looked like that probably thought most women wanted him.

"Are you a new client?"

That's great. He did think I was checking him out.

I looked back at the stunningly beautiful man. No way this man was some CEO of a tech company. Model, maybe.

I stuttered. "Um, no. I'm a podcaster." I cringed thinking I sounded more like a babbling idiot.

His eyes narrowed. "Oh, you're the podcaster here to interview Miranda. I hope you're not going to run poor Rebecca's memory into the ground."

I raised my hands defensively. "That's not my intention at all. Hopefully, you'll take a listen."

He smiled, but it wasn't a friendly smile. Something like annoyance, or was that anger, flashed in his eyes. "Miranda told me about your exclusive interview with Claude McKnight. Pathetic."

Who was he calling pathetic?

"Excuse me?"

"I'm sorry. He's a friend of yours." Ethan crooned as if he was consoling a child.

Even though he looked like a total snack, I decided right then and there that I didn't like him. It's a good thing Andre had warned me about him.

"Yes, he is." I managed a smile before saying, "Have a blessed day!"

Ethan studied me for a few more seconds. "I'm sure we will meet again, Joss Miller."

I hope not.

I took a deep breath as I heard his fancy shoes tap dance down the wooden staircase. So engrossed in Ethan's exit, I jumped when Angie said, "Ms. Miller, Miranda can see you now." Angie stepped from behind the curvy receptionist's desk. "Follow me and I will walk you back."

"Thank you." I fell in line behind Angie. We were about the same height. "The guy that left, was that Ethan Turner?"

Angie looked at me. "Yes, he comes in here often. One of our top clients."

Looked like more than a professional relationship to me.

I wondered if Ethan and Miranda discussed Rebecca's remains being found. How could they have a relationship and that not come up between them?

Angie knocked on the door and then opened it slightly. "I have... Oh, are you okay?" She quickly entered.

Not sure what to do, I followed.

Miranda sat behind her desk and wiped her face.

"Oh," I halted in the doorway. "Maybe I should come back."

"No, no. Sorry, it's been a lot." Miranda attempted to smile.

Angie frowned. "Are you sure you should be doing this? You don't have to talk to anyone about *her*."

I assumed Angie meant Rebecca.

Miranda came around the desk. "I've been looking forward to talking to Ms. Miller. I listened to your podcast from last season and the episode with Claude. You have quite a way with your interviewees."

I eased inside the office which faced the waterfront. "I appreciate you checking out the podcast and thank you for seeing me, Ms. Blackwell."

She waved at me. "Oh, call me Miranda. Did you want anything? Angie, honey, why don't you bring Joss, can I call you Joss... bring her a water for starters."

By the time I was seated, Angie appeared beside me with a bottled water.

"Thank you."

Angie gave me a look like I better not upset her sister and then closed the door.

Although she smiled at me, Miranda's eyes were still slightly red, and I wondered if she'd been crying for some time. "What a wonderfully unique way to present a true crime podcast. I grew up in Sugar Creek, but I wasn't aware of what happened to your grandfather."

Depending on which area of Sugar Creek one grew up, it's possible they never heard about my grandfather's murder. There was a time when the neighborhood where my grandmother lived was mostly a white neighborhood. Eugeena and her first husband had been one of the first Black families to move into the neighborhood. Now it was one of the more diverse areas of Charleston.

Instead of going into the history in my head, I quickly explained, "Many people haven't heard about his story, but he was greatly admired by his community."

Miranda's expression turned somber. "Like Rebecca. I still can't believe what happened to her. She was such a bright light, so talented and full of life. I miss her every day."

I nodded. "I can only imagine how difficult this must be for you, Miranda. I heard you were friends too."

Miranda's hazel eyes glistened with tears. When I first glimpsed her face, her eyes appeared green. With the sunlight shining through the window beside her desk, her eyes almost looked golden.

She smiled. "I'm surprised Claude talked to you. He's not an easy person to get in touch with. Rebecca tried to encourage him to work with me, but he didn't want the publicity."

"Claude and I are friends. He trusted me. I think it's important for people to hear from those who knew Rebecca best."

For a moment, Miranda looked hesitant. "You know we get a lot of requests for interviews. The phone was ringing off the hook when they found... her. And we had to call security on that awful man. What's his name?" Miranda snapped her fingers. "Landon? Lenny?"

I don't know why but I blurted. "Liam Holbrook?"

Miranda smacked her hand on the desk. "Yes. That's him. He's the worst, spreading his filthy rumors online."

"He was harassing Claude too. It's also why Claude decided to talk to me. He wanted to get his side of the story out in a safe way. You can tell from my podcasts that I'm not trying to tear anyone apart. I don't even call myself..." I held up my fingers and made air quotes, "...an investigator. I want people to know what Rebecca meant to the people around her."

A tear appeared in the corner of Miranda's eye. She reached over and snatched another tissue from the box on her desk. "Excuse me."

"I'm sorry for upsetting you."

"No, no. I'd be happy to do anything to help keep Rebecca's memory alive. And I want the person found who took her from us. We really miss her around here. Rebecca helped put Magnolia Media on the map."

Then, how did Miranda feel about Rebecca wanting to leave the agency?

Chapter 8
Relationships

COLD JUSTICE PODCAST

Season 2, Episode 2: The Publicist
Published: June 21

Joss: Welcome back to the *Cold Justice* Podcast. If you're tuning in for the second season, then you know I'm focusing on Rebecca Montgomery. The local artist's remains were recently identified earlier this week. On this episode, I will be speaking with someone who played a crucial role in Rebecca's professional life, her publicist, Miranda Blackwell.

As Rebecca's publicist, Miranda was responsible for promoting her work, arranging exhibitions and interviews, and helping to shape her public image. But beyond the business aspects of their relationship, Miranda became a trusted confidante and supporter, someone Rebecca could rely on through the ups and downs of her career and personal life.

This is the *Cold Justice* Podcast. Let's get into it!

Joss: Miranda, thank you so much for agreeing to this interview. I think it's important for our listeners to hear from those who knew Rebecca best. Can you start by telling us a little bit about your friendship with Rebecca?

Miranda: Of course, Joss. Rebecca and I met when she was starting out as an artist. She had so much raw talent, and I knew right away that I wanted to work with her. Over time, our professional relationship grew into a deep friendship. She was more than a client to me; she was a really good friend.

Joss: I can tell how much you admired her. What was it about Rebecca's art that spoke to you?

Miranda: Oh, Joss, where do I even begin? Rebecca had this way of infusing her work with so much emotion and meaning.

Every piece told a story, and I felt like I was getting a glimpse into her soul. She wasn't afraid to tackle difficult subjects or to use her art as a form of activism. It was truly inspiring.

Joss: I've heard that Rebecca was your first real client. Can you tell us a bit about what that was like, to work with her in those early days?

Miranda: Absolutely. When I first started Magnolia Media, I knew I wanted to focus on representing creatives. I'm not an artist myself, but I've always enjoyed art and music. Rebecca was so passionate about her work, and she was beautiful herself. She was a great storyteller and had such a bubbly personality. She could be shy, but once you got her talking about her latest creations, she was a star (sigh). It was an honor to watch her career take off.

Joss: Miranda, I know this might be difficult to talk about, but I have to ask. In light of recent events, do you have any thoughts on who might have harmed Rebecca?

Miranda: (pauses) Joss, I've thought about that a lot. The truth is, I don't know. It's hard for me to imagine anyone wanting to hurt her. I know the police are doing everything they can to find out what happened. We have to trust that process.

Joss: As her publicist, did you help her deal with any difficult people?

Miranda: Oh, well. Yes, there were occasions where some critic wrote a harsh piece or someone on social media wanted to start something to get new followers. But there were never any physical threats. At least I didn't see them. And if... Rebecca received any threats, she didn't share them with me. At the very least, I hope she would have told the police if she did.

Joss: Did you notice any changes in Rebecca's behavior or demeanor in the weeks leading up to her disappearance?

Miranda: (hesitates) Now that you mention it, there were a few things that seemed off. I thought it was because she was so focused on completing the mural for the Ashford Art Gallery. You know how artists are (laughs). When we did meet, she seemed distracted and anxious. I asked her if everything was okay, but she brushed it off. I... got the sense that maybe she was suffering from something mentally.

Joss: Why would you say that?

Miranda: She wanted a break from everything after she finished the *Black Girl Magic* mural. It was like she poured her whole self into that piece and it drained her. I don't know. She wanted to walk away.

Joss: She was leaving the agency?

Miranda: Not because she wasn't satisfied with us. She was tired. That's the best way I can describe it.

Joss: Rebecca was involved in a romantic relationship around the time of her disappearance. Were you aware of any problems in that relationship? Sometimes relationships can be draining.

Miranda: (long pause, then a sigh) I had a feeling this might come up (clears throat). Yes, it's well known *who* Rebecca was involved with. As a publicist to both, I have to say there was nothing unusual about their relationship. *He* was supportive of her.

(clears throat) And I should come clean, clear the air of any rumors. Grief is hard and it makes people grow closer. I can understand how it might raise some eyebrows if they see two people together out in public. It's been a comfort to have someone who understands what I'm going through (voice wavers). We both miss her every single day.

Joss: Thank you for clearing up any rumors. I have one last question. What do you think Rebecca's legacy will be, both as an artist and as a person?

Miranda: (takes a deep breath) I think Rebecca's legacy will be one of courage, compassion, and creativity. She used her art to shine a light on issues that mattered most to her, and she did it with such grace and honesty. I know her work will continue to inspire people for generations to come. As a person, Rebecca was kind, generous, and fiercely loyal. She made the world a better place, and I feel so lucky to have known her.

Joss: Thank you, Miranda. I know it isn't easy to talk about, but I believe it's so important to keep her spirit alive.

Miranda: Thank you, Joss, for giving me the opportunity to talk about my dear friend. I miss her every day, but I know that by sharing her story, we're ensuring that she'll never be forgotten.

Thursday, June 20, 8:37 p.m.

I decided to publish the second podcast interview early Friday morning. I'd gently pushed the limits of the interview by bringing up Ethan Turner, without really saying his name. Miranda did what I thought she would... she defended him and their relationship. Later after perusing her social media and his, I noticed a few pics of the couple. It wasn't that obvious, but I almost felt like Miranda used the opportunity to quell any rumors before they started, such as her budding relationship with Ethan and Rebecca's decision to leave the agency.

Miranda also validated what Claude had been trying to say.

I wondered if Rebecca was suffering from a mental breakdown.

I really wished, as Rebecca's publicist, that Miranda would have had more concrete examples of difficult people. But that would have made it too easy and I was sure the cops would have investigated someone who'd been harassing Rebecca.

I'd rushed home after begging Fay to let me leave a bit early. I didn't have to beg too hard, but I did promise to take on closing the café an extra day next week. My grandmother was dozing in her chair with Ginger in her lap and the tuxedo twins on the couch.

She smiled when I entered the living room. "You're home early today."

"I feel like I'm going to my second job. I'm going to work on the second interview and get it posted tomorrow."

"Oh, that sounds exciting. I made a chicken alfredo casserole. Be sure to heat up some before you get started," she said.

"Good idea. I'm starving."

With a bowl of food and a glass of sweet tea, I set up my MacBook on the kitchen table. The session with Nyla B last week helped me get back into the groove of making sure the levels were mixed right. The subscription for the new software was well worth it. I was happy I could do all this from the kitchen rather than having to go to the studio.

I'd spent my Christmas gift card from my mother on a nice pair of Bluetooth noise-canceling headphones. As I listened to Miranda's responses over and over again during the editing, I still couldn't get a good sense of her. I wondered how fans would feel about the interview and what their feedback would be, especially since she confessed her involvement with Ethan. Three years had passed since Rebecca went missing.

Still, I wondered if Ethan had strayed long before Rebecca's disappearance? Did Rebecca sense an attraction between her publicist and her boyfriend? Suppose that was the real reason Rebecca wanted to leave Miranda's agency? While Miranda's grief seemed genuine, I wondered if there was some guilt mixed in as well.

The interview produced more questions for me.

"There you are." A deep, familiar voice leaked through my headphones, scaring me out of my intense listen. I looked up to find my very handsome boyfriend staring down at me.

"Andre, I didn't hear you walk in." I pulled the headphones off my head.

Did the doorbell ring?

My grandmother came in behind him. "See, I told you she was hard at work on that podcast." She pointed to the pan of chicken alfredo on the stove. "Get you some dinner while you are here."

He grinned. "Thanks, Louise."

Andre had been here many times before and knew his way around my grandmother's kitchen.

"I'm surprised to see you." I looked at my phone and saw I had missed Andre's text.

"We've been missing each other this week." He pulled out a chair and sat down with a plate. Before taking a bite of the alfredo, he looked curiously at my setup. "What are you working on?"

"The second podcast episode. I interviewed Miranda Blackwell. I want it to come out tomorrow."

Andre's eyes widened slightly. "Two podcast episodes in one week."

"Yep, I figured I would keep the momentum going. Have you talked to her yet?"

"Miranda Blackwell. Rebecca's publicist?"

"Yes. "

"I have." Andre forked some chicken alfredo into his mouth.

While he chewed, I casually dropped. "So you know she's dating Ethan Turner?"

Andre placed his hand to his mouth and then swallowed. He looked at me. "No, I didn't. How do you know?"

"He was there this morning when I went to the office. Not a pleasant man."

Andre asked, "Did you talk to him?"

"Briefly. I guess Miranda told him I was coming. He knew my name. I could tell him and Claude have no love for each other."

"What did Miranda talk about?"

"I'm almost finished with the interview. You can be the first to listen to it. I edited some, but most of the responses I'm keeping. Nothing too controversial, still on a mission of keeping the listener sympathetic to who Rebecca Montgomery was."

"That's good." Andre nodded in approval.

"But you should know…"

Andre swiped a napkin from the holder on the table. After wiping his mouth, he crushed the used napkin. "I should have known you weren't going to make this easy, Joss."

I held my hands out in front of me to ward off any fussing. "I'm not investigating. But you should know that Rebecca was going to leave Magnolia Media. Rebecca was one of Miranda's first clients and they'd been working together for years."

Andre narrowed his eyes. "And Miranda told you all that?"

"I have a reputable source. But Miranda also mentioned that Rebecca seemed to be having a mental moment while working on that last mural."

He groaned like I'd hit him. "Wait, you have sources?"

I rolled my eyes. "Of course. Did you hear what I said?"

He nodded. "Yes, I've heard that people suspected Rebecca of having a mental illness. She did suffer from depression."

"Oh, that's good to know. But I wondered if Miranda and Ethan were involved long before Rebecca's disappearance. That could have affected her too. What do you think?"

He didn't say anything for a moment. Andre rubbed his chin, which had a lot more stubble than usual. "You're thinking that Rebecca would have been angry and depressed if she found out they were cheating."

"Claude said she was upset about something. Although, from what I've learned about Rebecca, I feel like she would have told Claude or Fay." I sighed. "Never mind. I saw some drama there and my thoughts started flying. There had to be someone that agitated Rebecca. Someone killed her."

My statement hung in the air as silence settled between us.

He pushed his empty plate away from him and leaned on the table. "Have you reached out to the sister yet?"

"Olivia? I've left some phone calls and sent emails. She hasn't reached back out yet."

Andre tilted his head. "Really? She's either called or been at the station almost every day since her sister's remains have been found."

"Can you blame her?"

He shook his head. "No, but if she does reach out to you, be weary of her. She's a lawyer. And you didn't hear this from me, but Olivia Montgomery has something to hide."

"Why do you say that? I know she admitted she and her sister didn't get along."

Andre crossed his arms. "It's what she hasn't been saying, and I have a sneaky suspicion it has to do with their mother's death. When she died, Olivia got everything."

I cocked my head. "Wait. Rebecca didn't get anything?"

"Olivia supposedly had power of attorney. From what I've heard, people think Olivia shut her younger sister out. Now she claims Rebecca had mental issues and couldn't handle being on her own. But I'm not buying it. Rebecca was fine financially."

I frowned. "Sounds like Olivia was greedy. Fay always thought Olivia was jealous."

"I'm not saying she's not genuine, but I read people pretty well. There's guilt there. Maybe it's because she didn't appreciate her sister while she was alive. I don't really know. But Olivia Montgomery is a tricky woman to watch. Like I said, beware when talking to her." Andre stood, leaned over and kissed me. "Go to sleep soon. Don't let this podcast take over your life. Two podcasts in one week, Joss."

"I have to get on it while it's hot."

"Mmmm. I'm going to go. Suddenly feels hot in here for other reasons."

I grinned. I loved when Andre flirted like this. But I also knew if he didn't leave, we were both going to be in trouble.

It was my grandmother's house. That thought put a damper on my hormones as I walked him out.

At least for a little while.

Chapter 9
Spilling the Tea

Sunday, June 23, 1:54 p.m.

There was a time in my life where I didn't have many places to go. Life could be rather dull for me. Today, I had choices. The Pattersons were having Sunday dinner and my grandmother had decided to attend. My great aunts also had called to see if I could stop by. I ended up begging my grandmother to bring me a plate from the Pattersons and took a rain check with my great aunts.

I was going to a tea party.

This would be a first for me.

As promised, Eleanor got me an invite to the Sunday Afternoon Tea event at the Ashford Art Gallery. My only concept of a tea party stemmed from reading *Alice in Wonderland* when I was younger. I was sure the gallery's tea party would be more civilized without the rabbit always running late or the Mad Hatter.

I was pretty excited about stepping inside the infamous Ashford Art Gallery for the first time. Like most of my potential podcast guests, I'd researched the gallery owner last night. Vivian Ashford had quite an extensive biography and tons of press clippings. The gallery's website had a section about the artists currently on display.

There were several articles written around the time the mural Rebecca painted was revealed to the public. There were pictures I'd never seen before of Rebecca standing with Vivian and many other guests who came to view the mural.

I wondered how Vivian selected the artists she featured in her gallery. How did she become aware of Rebecca Montgomery? What influenced her to commission Rebecca to paint the famous mural in the gallery?

The last mural that Rebecca would ever create.

I'd written questions in a notebook in case I had an opportunity to talk to the charismatic owner. Rebecca had spent the majority of her time at the gallery up until the mural's reveal. Three days later, she went missing. I hoped to get a sense of what might have been happening behind the scenes for her.

Eleanor asked if I wanted to ride with her, but I preferred my own vehicle, in case I needed to get away quickly. Guided by the familiar voice from the Google Maps app on my phone, I drove past the building and followed the gallery signs. There were plenty of parking spaces since it was Sunday, but when I pulled my seven year old Honda Civic alongside Mercedes, BMWs and Audis, I immediately felt out of place.

I wasn't sure what to wear and opted for an off the shoulder pantsuit. It was a pretty bold purchase from a year ago that I'd never worn. I often didn't wear white. But I liked this outfit with its light gold streaks that shimmered in the sunlight. The pants were pretty comfortable and ballooned out around my legs. I had a bad habit of making impulsive purchases. But the gold sandals I dug out from a shoe box were perfect.

Eleanor mentioned hats were highly recommended for the tea party. I sat in my car gawking at women with fancy hats that would have made my great aunts proud. Thankfully, there were as many simple hats as intricately designed ones.

I wasn't really a hat person, but today instead of sporting my usual afro puff, I let my curls sprout from my head. The straw hat I donned for the event today, I'd purchased for Easter a few years ago. I liked the way it tilted down slightly over my face and the silk interior protected my curls. It was my go to whenever I hit the beach.

I climbed out of my well-worn baby and headed up the sidewalk behind a group of women. I'd never seen Eleanor's car before, so I didn't know if she had arrived yet. The author seemed to magically show up inside the café on a regular basis. I knew she didn't live far and walked.

"Joss."

I heard my name and swung right and then left trying to locate the familiar voice.

Eleanor appeared ahead waving at me. She was wearing a pale blue coatdress. It occurred to me that as much as I saw the writer, I'd never seen her in a dress. She wore a floppy blue hat which made me feel better about my beach hat.

"You made it." Eleanor offered me a hug.

"I did. Thank you for getting me in. I've never been inside."

"Really? That's surprising since you are surrounded by artists." Eleanor stated.

That was true. Between Fay, Claude, Briana, Nyla, and a host of others, I was always around artists and musicians. Walking through the glass doors of the Ashford Art Gallery was like walking into another side of the art world.

A sophisticated and posh side.

The sounds of excited feminine voices and heels clicking across the shiny bright marble floor greeted us on the other side of the double door entrance.

"Brace yourself." Eleanor whispered. "You're about to experience Rebecca's last piece of work." As we drew closer, Eleanor exclaimed. "Oh my, there usually aren't this many people in the gallery on Sundays."

I'd never been in here so I didn't know what to expect. I could tell some of the people milling around were not here for the tea party. In fact, I glimpsed the infamous Liam Holbrook attempting to talk to people. Most gave him a look and stepped around him. He was in the way of the actual show. Well, not really a show, but the mural was breathtaking.

I stopped in my tracks and took in the piece. I'd seen only parts and pieces online. In its full glory was the mural known as *Black Girl Magic* by Rebecca Montgomery. I recognized the area of the mural where Rebecca last stood in the gallery. It was emblazoned on my brain since I'd seen that particular photo dozens of times.

Despite the crowd of gawkers, I stepped up to view the mural up close. The sheer scale and power of it left me awestruck. Rebecca's work outside the Lofts was stunning against the old brick, but this was vibrant color against what once was a stark white wall.

The 20-foot tall mural depicted a regal Black woman emerging from a fiery solar flare, her arms outstretched, palms open as if conjuring galaxies. Her skin was painted in rich shades of deep mahogany, highlighted with swirls of shimmering gold. Stars and planets seemed to orbit around her. The details of her face conveyed both serenity and fierce strength. But it was the vivid dark strokes that formed the mass of curls around her face that made me smile.

I was very proud to be a Black woman.

I glanced around. There were other "sisters" with that same proud look on their face.

When I went to work tomorrow, I would love to know how Fay felt about her friend's work. It was a bold, stirring piece, and it made me want to meet Vivian even more.

Eleanor tapped my shoulder. "It's incredible, isn't it? The doors are opening for the tea and we want to get good seats."

As I followed Eleanor down another hallway, I looked up and caught sight of Liam looking at me. I smiled and waved.

He didn't return my greeting, but instead moved on to find another victim he could talk to. I imagined he wasn't happy with me releasing a second episode of the podcast only days after the first. When I did the first season, I had all the episodes done so I could release them at the same time. This time was a bit different, but I knew how fickle and quick people forgot about content since there was such an overwhelming amount out there.

I could sort of relate to Liam's need to keep feeding the machine. He did say he had sponsors so I guess his brand was how he made his living. I appreciated working at the café and having the podcast as my side hobby for now. Right now I hoped this tea party would provide another opportunity for future podcast episodes.

Or I was going to have a short season two.

Eleanor and I stopped outside an open door behind a line of women, some dressed in their Sunday best, others in pantsuits and jumpsuits. All with hats. When we finally stepped inside, once again I felt like I'd walked into something magical.

The view was not as stunning as the *Black Girl Magic* mural, but it was special. Large windows framed a view of the Charleston skyline and waterfront. Tables with seats for up to four occupants were scattered around the room. On the side wall, the line that had entered began to wrap around a table of food.

On cue, my stomach rumbled, reminding me that the bagel I'd eaten earlier that morning had long been consumed. We reached the table, and I was surprised. The plates were real ceramic, not paper plates. Utensils were wrapped snug inside black napkins.

I whispered to Eleanor. "Are these always this fancy?"

Eleanor chuckled. "Vivian is British. She loves the formality of these tea gatherings. Nothing but the best from her."

"I see." I grabbed the plate, which wasn't lightweight at all. There was a smorgasbord of food. I filled my plate with fresh grapes, strawberries and kiwi. Then continued, adding cheeses, crackers, and some crustless sandwiches. Of course this was a tea party. Perpendicular to the food tables were a row of cups and actual tea pots. There was also iced tea as well.

We found a table off to the side. One thing I knew about Eleanor from her office hours at the café, the writer loved observing people. That was definitely what I wanted to do. As I munched, I didn't see anyone I knew other than Eleanor.

"Oh, here comes Vivian." Eleanor tipped her head in the direction to my right.

I turned slightly in my chair and watched the gallery owner make her way toward us. She navigated the crowd with the ease of someone accustomed to being the center of attention.

A LATTE MAYHEM

Pausing occasionally to greet other guests, she exchanged both air kisses and brief pleasantries.

As expected, Vivian appeared regal. I assumed she was Eleanor's age, but with her slim figure, she could have passed for younger. I couldn't afford designer clothing, but the tailored cream suit adorned with a long string of pearls looked expensive. Her silver hair was styled in a sleek bob that framed her angular face.

She must have spotted Eleanor. Switching directions with ease, she headed toward our table. I don't know why but I found myself dabbing my mouth with my napkin, hoping I didn't have anything on my face.

"Eleanor, so good to see you."

Eleanor stood to embrace the woman. I watched as Vivian stepped back and clasped Eleanor's hands. "You've been missing in action for quite a few of these. How's the book coming?"

Eleanor laughed. "Well, the last one is with the editor. I've started something new. A new series in fact." She glanced over at me. "I told you I was bringing a friend today."

Vivian's gaze landed on me, her eyes bright. "You must be Joss," she said, her accent a refined London lilt. "Eleanor has told me about your podcast. I'm so glad you could join us today."

I stood to shake her hand, feeling a bit intimidated. "Thank you for having me, Vivian. I was admiring the *Black Girl Magic* mural outside. It's truly stunning to see in person."

A flash of emotion flickered across Vivian's face. "Yes, it was Rebecca's crowning achievement. A true testament to her talent and vision." She paused, seeming to gather herself. "I do hope you'll consider interviewing me for your podcast, Joss. I think it's important that Rebecca's story be told. She deserves to be remembered for the brilliant artist and beautiful soul she was."

I stuttered. "Yes, I would be honored, Vivian. Thank you for the opportunity."

She winked at me. "We'll talk soon."

As Vivian turned to greet another guest, I caught Eleanor's eye. She was grinning as hard as I knew I was. I didn't even have to ask. The woman volunteered to be on my little ole podcast.

Thank you, Lord!

I was truly grateful at how this was all coming together. It felt like it was meant for me to tell the story of Rebecca's life without the current exploitation happening in the news and on social media.

I was basking in the glow when I noticed a hush fell over the room. I looked up and caught Eleanor's gaze fixed on something or someone behind me.

I turned to see a woman striding purposefully toward Vivian. I recognized her from the news reports. Olivia Montgomery, Rebecca's sister.

I exchanged a look with Eleanor. "Does Olivia usually come to these events?"

Eleanor shook her head, her face awash in concern. "I don't think so. Olivia has lashed out at a number of people, including Vivian. I have no idea why she's here."

Something was clearly on the woman's mind as she stopped in front of Vivian.

Sunday, June 23, 2:36 p.m.

Olivia's posture was so rigid, she looked like she might snap. Why was she so angry and why be confrontational in a public place? I could understand her being upset about her sister, but this felt unhinged.

Vivian hadn't walked far from us, so it wasn't hard to hear Olivia hiss. "How dare you?"

The gallery owner stepped back, grabbing at the string of pearls hanging around her neck. "Olivia. It's good to see you. Do you want to talk in my office?"

Olivia kept right on talking as if she didn't hear Vivian's question. "You're benefiting off my sister's work. You should be ashamed of yourself."

Vivian's eyes widened, a mix of shock and indignation flashing across her face. "What exactly are you accusing me of? Your sister put her heart and soul into that piece."

"And she's gone." Olivia snapped, cutting her off. "You know something. Something was wrong the entire time she worked on that piece. And you're here with your superficial tea party instead of helping find who did this. You probably know who killed her."

The room had gone deathly silent. I glanced at Eleanor, who looked as stunned as I felt.

Vivian drew herself up to her full height, her British accent made her sound formal and in control. "I have told the police everything I know, Olivia. I am as devastated by Rebecca's loss as you are."

Olivia let out a bitter laugh. "Devastated? You introduced her to a whole new world of people. And you're telling me you have no idea what happened?"

Vivian's face crumpled. "I wish I did, Olivia. I wish I had some answers for you. Rebecca was so special to me. I would do anything to have her back."

Olivia's voice rose. "If you truly cared about Rebecca, you'd be doing everything in your power to find out what happened to her. Instead, you're carrying on with your little tea parties and extravagant galas, celebrating the tragedy of a talented artist. Somebody did this. Rebecca had her issues, but she'd spiraled from the moment she started working on that—"

Olivia threw up her hand, turned on her heel, and stalked out of the gallery. I glimpsed the pain etched on her face. I couldn't tell if it was genuine or all for show. She could have talked to Vivian privately.

Why come here and make a spectacle of herself?

The stunned silence in the room lingered after Olivia's exit. Vivian, who had been staring after Olivia, blinked as if to shake off what happened. "Ladies," she said to the room, "I'm so sorry for that interruption. Ms. Montgomery is understandably upset about her sister. Please do continue your tea and conversations. I know that Rebecca would want us to remember her."

I looked at Eleanor, my mind racing. Olivia's accusations had opened up a whole new avenue of questions. Could Vivian be hiding something? I wondered if I should change up my questions. It sounded like Rebecca may have met some people through Vivian. Was Olivia grasping at straws trying to point fingers at anyone associated with her sister?

I guess it was a good thing Olivia was no longer focused on Claude.

As the murmurs of the crowd started to build again, I knew one thing for certain – I was doing what Andre didn't want me to do.

I really wanted to investigate what happened to Rebecca.

Sunday, June 23, 4:05 p.m.

The chatter in the room gradually resumed. I discovered this event was more than about tea. It was an art gallery. A composed Vivian continued with her event introducing two new female artists, one a painter and the other a sculptor. Guests were escorted to sneak peeks of new exhibits featuring the new artists and had an opportunity to greet them.

Eleanor hugged me. "I've had enough excitement for the day. I talked to Vivian and mentioned that she should come talk to you. Let me know if everything works out or I will keep my eyes open for your next episode."

"Thanks, Eleanor, for everything."

I waited around for a while, touring the various exhibits in the gallery until Vivian approached me.

"Joss, I apologize for that scene with this being your first time at one of these events. Olivia is understandably grieving, but her accusations are unfounded. I would never do anything to harm Rebecca. As you can see, I support artists, especially women."

"Yes, I see you have many wonderful artists on display. Did you introduce Rebecca like this on a Sunday afternoon?"

Vivian beamed. "I did. We announced that she would be creating a mural here in the gallery. By that time, many people were already familiar with her murals at the Lofts and at Synaptic. The announcement created quite the buzz, and she was so excited."

I nodded. "If you're willing, I'd still love to interview you for my podcast. That mural is Rebecca's last work. It's very special."

Vivian hesitated a moment before nodding. "Yes, of course. Give me a few minutes to greet some more guests and check in with my staff." She smiled. "Then we can talk in my office. Eleanor has told me many good things about you and I look forward to your questions."

Vivian disappeared into the crowd, and I took the opportunity to study the *Black Girl Magic* mural once more. What had Rebecca been going through while working on this piece? From her sister's outburst, she also seemed to think, like a few others, that something had transpired while Rebecca worked on this artistic masterpiece.

Lost in thought, I didn't notice Liam sidling up beside me until he spoke, his voice low and close to my ear. "Quite the drama, wasn't it? I managed to capture the whole thing on my phone. This is going to make for some great content for *Shady Affairs*."

Startled, I took a step back, putting some distance between us. "You can't exploit people's pain for views. This is a real tragedy, not some sensationalized story for your followers. Olivia is obviously hurting over her sister's death."

Liam's eyes gleamed with a predatory intensity as he looked me up and down. "Come on. You and I both know that in this business it's all about giving the people what they want.

And what they want is the juicy details, the scandal, the raw emotion."

I crossed my arms, feeling increasingly uncomfortable under his gaze. "Well, I won't stoop to that level, no matter how many views it might get me."

Liam took a step closer, his smirk widening. "You are quite the goody two shoes, aren't you."

I flinched. "I wouldn't say that. I just have a different way of telling a story."

His gaze was really intense. "Anyone ever tell you that you look like Rebecca?"

What is wrong with this guy?

We had similar complexions, but we didn't look that much alike.

As I was about to respond, Vivian appeared beside us, her expression stern. "Mr. Holbrook, I don't believe you were invited to this event. I have a strict media list. How exactly did you get in?"

Liam's smirk faltered and anger sparked in his eyes. "There's no need to be insulting. And I'm pretty sure I am on your list."

Vivian's eyes narrowed. "*Shady Affairs*. I know of what you do, Mr. Holbrook, and it does not represent the fine arts world.

Be that as it may, I must ask you to leave. This is a private event, and I won't have you harassing my guests."

Liam snarled. "I was just leaving anyway. I got what I needed." He turned to me, his gaze lingering. "Until next time, Joss."

With that, Liam sauntered off, leaving me feeling both relieved and unsettled. Vivian placed a comforting hand on my shoulder. "I apologize for that, Joss. Liam Holbrook has a reputation for being a bit of a vulture. I hope he didn't make you too uncomfortable."

I shook my head, trying to dispel the uneasy feeling that had settled over me. "I'm alright, Vivian. Thank you for intervening. I appreciate it."

Vivian nodded, her expression softening. "Of course, dear. Now, why don't we head to my office? I believe we have an interview to conduct."

I followed Vivian toward her office. I wasn't going to let shady Liam or anyone else distract me from that goal.

Chapter 10
Smear Campaign Starts

COLD JUSTICE PODCAST

Season 2, Episode 3: Black Girl Magic
Published: June 24

Joss: Hello, listeners. Welcome back to the *Cold Justice* Podcast. In today's episode, we'll be exploring Rebecca Montgomery's life and work through the eyes of someone who knew her well - Vivian Ashford, the owner of the Ashford Art Gallery.

Vivian and Rebecca's paths first crossed four years ago after Rebecca painted a mural for the tech company Synaptic. Vivian commissioned Rebecca to create a mural for the Ashford Art Gallery. I had a chance to see this stunning piece of art called *Black Girl Magic*. It made me so proud to see Rebecca's last work up close.

Now, three years after Rebecca's mysterious disappearance and the finding of her remains, Vivian is opening up about her memories of the young artist. In this intimate conversation, we'll be exploring the person behind the mural and learning more about the legacy Rebecca left behind.

This is the *Cold Justice* Podcast. Let's get into it!

Joss: Vivian, thank you so much for agreeing to this interview. Can you tell me about the first time you met Rebecca?

Vivian: I was visiting with Ethan Turner's company.

Joss: Synaptic?

Vivian: Yes. He has an open house there each year where he invites a select few to see the latest innovations they have coming out. I sit on the board and have known Ethan from his humble beginnings, actually since he was a wee child (laughs).

I'm his aunt by marriage. Ethan's mother was my husband's only sibling.

Anyway, he told me he was renovating the office space he'd acquired. It's not too far from my gallery. Beautiful older building. He had to be particular about not disturbing the historical architecture on the outside too much, but he did wonders with modernizing the inside.

Joss: One of those additions was a mural in the lobby. What was your reaction when you first saw the mural?

Vivian: The first time I saw the mural, I was absolutely stunned. The scale, the colors, the emotion - it was breathtaking. I remember standing there thinking who is this artist. Later, Ethan introduced me to Rebecca. They weren't dating at the time, but later on they became a couple.

Joss: What made you decide to commission Rebecca to create the *Black Girl Magic* mural for your gallery?

Vivian: After seeing the mural at Synaptic, I knew I wanted to work with Rebecca on a larger scale. I approached her about creating a piece for the front of my gallery - something that would make a statement and celebrate the strength and beauty of Black women. Rebecca was hesitant at first, but I could see the wheels turning in her head. I think she was excited by the challenge.

Joss: How long did she work on it? That must have been hard to keep under wraps with the gallery remaining open.

Vivian: Oh goodness! It was a process. She told me she went through many, many sketches before she settled on one to show me. It was just a black and white sketch, but I knew once she painted it with the vibrant colors she so loved, that it would be stunning. We had to build a structure around the wall. It had a door with a lock and everything. It was such an exciting time, those few months. She would come every morning and sometimes be here late at night.

Joss: How did Rebecca feel leading up to the unveiling of the mural?

Vivian: SShe was a bundle of nerves in the weeks leading up to the premiere. She put so much of herself into that mural, and I think she felt extremely vulnerable putting it out there for the world to see. She kept making tiny adjustments, the perfectionist that she was. The night of the unveiling, she was practically shaking. But when the curtain dropped and she saw the reactions of the crowd —the tears, the cheers, the awe—I watched a sense of peace and pride wash over her. She knew she had created something special.

Joss: Rebecca's disappearance and death shocked the community. How did you feel when you heard the news?

A LATTE MAYHEM

Vivian: I was absolutely devastated when I heard about Rebecca's disappearance. We'd had the mural reveal and she was so thrilled. We'd gotten to know each other those few months. I held out hope that she would be found safe, but as the days stretched on, a sense of dread settled in my gut (silence). When they identified those remains as her, I felt like I had lost a daughter. The grief was overwhelming. And it's been compounded by the mystery around her death. I don't understand why someone would hurt her.

Joss: Vivian, there have been rumors. Do you have any insight into Rebecca's state of mind during the time she was working on the mural at your gallery? Was it more than just nerves?

Vivian: (takes a deep breath) I was aware that Rebecca was going through a difficult time, but I didn't realize the extent of it. She'd taken the death of her mother hard. We had a conversation about it once.

There were nights when she would work late at the gallery. I would check on her before I left for the evening, find her sitting in front of the mural, lost in thought. One evening, she confided in me that she felt like she was being watched. I told her these old historic buildings creak and moan at night. I've experienced the same feeling after dark or when I'm here by myself.

I tried to reassure her and I made sure to change the security codes and increase the surveillance around the gallery, just to be safe (pauses). Looking back, I wish I had done more to help her. Maybe I should have insisted she go to the police, but she did say she wasn't sure if it was in her mind or not.

Joss: Maybe it wasn't in her mind. As you think back to the time when Rebecca was working on the mural, do you recall noticing anyone unusual or suspicious hanging around the gallery or paying particular attention to Rebecca?

Vivian: (pauses to think) You know, it's been almost three years, and we have so many tourists and visitors coming in and out of the gallery all the time. It's hard to pinpoint any specific individuals who might have stood out.

However, now that you mention it, there was a period of a few weeks when I noticed a homeless man who camped out near the entrance.

Joss: Was that unusual?

Vivian: Well, we have a growing population of homeless people. I saw it on the news. But this man stayed in the corner of the building. He never came inside, but I would see him loitering across the street or sitting on the bench near the entrance.

I wish I could give you a better description, but it was so long ago, and I wasn't really paying close attention. I'll definitely give it some more thought and let you know if anything else comes to mind.

Joss: Did he just go away?

Vivian: I did stop seeing him. But it could be that someone asked him to leave. Some businesses are concerned for their customers and tourists. I'm not sure why I thought of that now. Maybe her ... being found has me thinking a lot.

Joss: That's understandable. Is there anything else you'd like to share about Rebecca?

Vivian: I want people to remember Rebecca for the incredible artist and person she was. She had a vision for a better world and the talent to bring that vision to life. Her murals weren't just paint on a wall—they were a call to action, a call for change. I hope that her legacy will continue to inspire and challenge us all. Rebecca Montgomery was one of a kind, and she will be deeply missed.

Tuesday, June 25, 6:14 p.m.

Liam stuck to his word. He released the camera footage of Olivia telling Vivian off in front of her guests. Other social media sites that simply reposted whatever *Shady Affairs* published spread the smear campaign.

And apparently, I was on his hit list too. On a roll, Liam published a post bad-mouthing me and my podcast. At last count, the video had over 100,000 views. Not nearly as many as the 500,000 views of Olivia's outburst. But it was enough.

Andre wanted to arrest him.

Fay wanted to ban him from the café.

I wasn't sure what I wanted to do to him, but I had a feeling if we were face-to-face, I'd have a hard time not telling him where he and his *Shady Affairs* platform could go.

For probably the fourth or fifth time today, I played the video. This time I looked at the background where Liam did his latest rant. He wasn't in his car, he appeared to be inside his bedroom. There was a bed behind him with rumpled bedsheets.

Did this guy just jump out of bed and start venting?

Liam spoke directly to the camera with a frustrated expression. His usual combed hair stuck up around his head as if he'd been trying to pull it out. When I first saw this video it upset me, but the more I looked at it, Liam appeared unhinged to me.

"Hey everyone, Liam here from *Shady Affairs*. I've got some tea to spill about this *Cold Justice* podcast. I mean can it really be called a podcast?

"Now, I've been hearing a lot of buzz about the interviews, and some of you have been asking me, 'Liam, how does Joss Miller get such juicy scoops?' Well, I'll tell you how. Joss is a barista masquerading as a journalist. That's right, folks. When she's not pretending to be a hard-hitting reporter, she's slinging lattes at a local coffee shop.

"But wait, there's more. I've got some inside information that Ms. Miller has been cozying up to a certain Detective Andre Baez. Yeah, one of the detectives on the Rebecca Montgomery case. Coincidence? I think not. It's clear that she's using her personal relationship to get the inside track on the case. It's a classic case of 'who you know' rather than actual talent or hard work.

"I mean, really, she's not even investigating. She had Claude McKnight talking about his friendship – so what. The facts are he argued with Rebecca before she died. And he was the last person to see her alive. Then, the next episode is with the publicist. Who by the way is sleeping with Ethan Turner. That, my friends, is shady stuff.

The latest. Vivian Ashford. I'm not even sure why that woman had anything to say. She's basking in the attention from the mural Rebecca Montgomery painted. But my sources say Rebecca was upset at that gala. Maybe she regretted painting the mural. Who knows.

"Anyway, don't be fooled by Ms. Miller and her supposed 'exclusives.' Stick with *Shady Affairs* for the real scoop. I promise to always dig deep and bring you the unfiltered truth, no matter what.

"Finding the shade, my friends. I'm out."

Liam winked at the camera before ending the video.

Then his rant started all over again.

"Are you watching *that* again?" Fay said.

I shrugged, placing the phone back in my pocket. "I'm okay. It's how Liam makes his living. I had a feeling he didn't like that I turned down his offer to partner. And while I've been blessed with getting interviews, he's been failing miserably."

Fay shook her head. "That's no reason for him to call you out on social media. Those folks trusted you enough to let you post their interviews. You didn't twist around what they said or try to exploit them for followers."

"No, but I'm attracting attention. You know the first season of the podcast, people wanted to connect me to a woman's murder." I frowned. "Now, I'm talking about a woman's murder."

Fay opened a box of cups she'd taken out of storage. "It's true crime and you're shedding light on Becca's humanity. People are too busy wanting to speculate and get likes for their posts. She was a fantastic person and artist. I really appreciate that you are doing this."

I took the stack of cups Fay passed to me and started placing them on the counter. "Are you sure you don't want to be on the podcast?"

Fay smiled. "I think you have the best people so far. That was really nice, the things Vivian said about Becca. She's a class act. Who else are you thinking about getting?"

"After seeing her go in on Vivian this past Sunday, I still wouldn't mind talking to Olivia."

Fay glanced at me as she pulled out the empty trays from the shelves. "I told you to be wary of her."

I went behind her and grabbed the other trays. Fay liked having fresh baked goods every morning. She didn't have any problem selling out. Any leftovers, she passed along or let us take them home. Probably one of the reasons why my hips had become shapely. I'd already put some blueberry muffins and chocolate chip cookies to the side.

"I know, but she's so all over the place. I feel like she wants to know what happened to her sister. The only other person I could try to interview is Ethan Turner. And Andre has warned me to stay away from him."

Fay arched an eyebrow. "Really. Any ideas why?"

I grimaced. "I shouldn't say any more. Sometimes Andre talks to me about work, not always though. He's a professional."

"Of course he is." Fay stacked the trays. "It's fine if he does talk to you. You are partners. He probably needs someone to vent to sometimes." She tilted her head with a slight smirk on her face. "And if Andre is leaning toward Ethan, I wouldn't be surprised. I never understood what Becca saw in him."

"Did she confide in you about him?"

Fay shook her head. "No. But that's what was so weird. Me and her always got together and talked about our relationships. She was my rock when I was going through my divorce. I vented to her all the time. She even let me stay with her for a bit until I got my own place. With her past relationships, she would do the same. Share all her gripes and anxieties. But with Ethan, I didn't even know they were dating. The one time I met him, he barely acknowledged me when Becca introduced me. A real icy kind of guy, even if he is good looking. I'm sure it's because I wasn't his type."

Fay grabbed the trays off the counter and walked into the back.

I followed her with the remaining trays. "He has a type?"

"Oh yeah." Fay looked at me up and down. "Actually, I can see why Andre told you to stay away from him. I hadn't noticed this before, but you favor Becca a little. It's the complexion and the curly hair. Before Becca started her locs, she wore her hair like yours, in an afro puff. You both have similar styles in clothing. A bit bohemian, a little eclectic."

I wrinkled my nose. "That's supposed to be Ethan's type? He's dating her publicist, Miranda Blackwell. She's far from either of us."

Fay whipped her head around and stared. "Is that so? You know I told Becca once that woman had her eyes on Ethan. She finally got him, huh? I can guarantee you he's with her because she makes him look good, but she's not his type either."

I didn't try to argue with Fay. Oftentimes, she was right.

"So you knew most of the other guys Rebecca was involved with?"

"Not all of them." Fay placed the empty trays in the industrialized dishwasher she had installed earlier this year. "There was a period of time when she dated online, something I never liked to do. She would tell me about the guys she dated, but none of them stuck past a couple of dates. There were one or two guys she dated for longer than two years, one was in school with us."

I grabbed the broom out of the closest and started sweeping around the kitchen area. "What happened?"

Fay sighed. "Unfortunately, he died in a motorcycle accident. If I had to guess, Tommy Vick was the love of Becca's life. He was nineteen at the time of his accident, but I believe those two would have gotten married."

My heart dropped. "Oh, that's so sad."

Fay pressed the button on the machine to start the wash cycle. "Yeah, Becca stayed with the next guy for about three or four years. Rob McCawley. Rob was a blue collar guy. Worked down at the ports. He claimed he loved Becca, but he came from a large family and wanted one of his own. He'd proposed to her, but Becca wasn't ready. Rob ended things and moved on. He broke her heart. "

I swept up the pile of dirt I'd gathered onto the dustpan. "Wow, he could have waited."

Fay nodded. "Absolutely! If he loved her. He knew art was important to her. She really wanted to prove to her mom that she could make it with her art." Fay pulled the clip out of her hair and let her dreads fall down to her shoulders. "It didn't help Becca that her older sister was the ultimate overachiever. Going off to law school and all. Becca even left Charleston for a while to get away from her mom and sister hounding her."

"Really? Where did she go?"

Fay walked into her office and sat down. "Savannah, Georgia. She'd gone to SCAD, Savannah College of Art and Design and later went back to teach for a while. It was good for her. We still kept in touch. I know she dated someone there too. But we caught up so irregularly during that time, I can't say I remember anything about him."

I perked up at this news. "I have a friend who teaches at SCAD. She's Nyla B's older sister. I'll check to see if they knew each other."

Fay nodded. "Becca came back about a year before her mom passed. She died about five years ago from breast cancer. Although Olivia would like to make it seem like she did all the work, the sisters took turns taking care of their mom. I remember Becca caring for their mother as well. It's really sad how

Olivia treated her own sister. It's not like they have extended family. They only have... had each other."

"I'm sure you saw the video Liam grabbed. Olivia blamed Vivian for not doing enough to find out what happened to her sister. Even accused her of knowing what happened. Was Olivia always that confrontational?"

Fay sucked in her teeth. "Oh yeah! That's Olivia. She likes being the center of attention. She blames everyone for Rebecca's death, but she abandoned her own sister after their mother died. Somehow she managed to get control of all their mom's finances and property. If anything, Olivia is probably feeling guilty."

"I can imagine." I went over and grabbed my stuff out of my locker. It was always easier to close up the café when two people worked together. Tomorrow was my day off and I intended to actually rest.

Fay and I walked toward the café entrance. "If she does contact you, be careful. She tries to play on people's sympathy, but I listened to Becca vent enough. Olivia was jealous of her sister's easygoing, free spirit. If I'm honest, Becca was the prettier one of the two. Never had a problem catching men. Olivia is about four years older, but the way she acts and carries herself, you would almost think she was ten to fifteen years older. Becca

A LATTE MAYHEM

often told me if Olivia had her way, she would have preferred to stay an only child."

I stepped out into the humid air. "That's pretty sad. Do you think she's genuine about finding out who killed her sister?"

Fay closed the door and locked it before turning around to face me. "I'm not saying she's not. I just know the sisters weren't close. In her own way, maybe Olivia misses her sister. But the woman I see doing all these interviews, in my opinion, she kind of likes that attention."

We walked across the street to our cars. Fay had me wondering. My older brother was almost five years older and only occasionally reached out. I loved him as much as I did when I was a little girl riding around on his back. I don't think he stopped caring about me and mom. He was just doing his own thing. Living life the way he wanted. If we really needed him, I believed he would come home.

At least I hoped.

I waved to Fay before swinging my car out the parking lot. In my rearview mirror, I watched her pull out and drive off in the opposite direction. Even though she was my boss, Fay had become like an older sister to me. We looked out for each other.

I wondered why Olivia didn't look out more for her younger sister.

And where was her guilt really coming from?

Chapter 11
Guilty Party

Wednesday, June 26, 12:08 a.m.

I stayed up waiting for Andre to call. Or text.

This was not unusual for me when I was in a relationship. The only difference was Andre did respond. No matter the time of night. I'd become accustomed to being mistreated by the opposite sex that I couldn't believe it at first. Fay and Leesa told me his responding was a good sign. A sign of what, I wasn't sure. But I liked it.

So while I waited, I wasn't fretting quite as bad as I had in the past.

Like any large city, crime was a part of the fabric in Charleston, meaning homicide stayed busy. Andre had more cases than he could keep up with besides Rebecca Montgomery. Some were a lot fresher, requiring his attention over the colder cases.

While I was interviewing Vivian, my boyfriend had been called to the scene of a domestic crime. It was pretty sad from what I gleaned from the news report and what Andre shared later. A woman who was being stalked by her ex had reached out to the police for a restraining order. Defying the order, the man shot her while she was getting ready to go out with friends. One of the friends was also shot.

I'd never dreamed I would have a boyfriend who was a cop, and definitely not a homicide detective. I'd read and watched enough crime shows to know that kind of life was tough on a relationship. I tried not to worry, and even if we couldn't spend time together, I was glad he stayed in touch. I knew he lived a dangerous life.

It was scary!

So I didn't overthink, I busied myself with tasks for the podcast. First, I needed to figure out what to do with Liam Holbrook and his *Shady Affairs* trolls. A glutton for punishment, I watched the infamous video again. At this point it was more constructive criticism to me. If I had to boast about my strengths, this girl knew how to squeeze positivity out of anything negative.

One of my favorite bible stories as a little girl was the story of Joseph. After all that man went through, he kept it positive and knew God had his back. I liked to think I was mature enough to glean lessons from a turd like Liam Holbrook.

Plus, I had a pretty good following of almost 5,000 people, not that I was counting. I was grateful. From the comments under my posts, fifty percent of the people appreciated what I was doing. Another twenty-five percent actually knew Rebecca and left their own comments about missing her.

Then there were the rest who definitely had to be Liam's tribe.

ShadyAffairsFanatic: Stick to serving coffee. Liam is right, Joss is just riding on her detective boyfriend's coattails. He hasn't even found the killer yet.

PodcastPolice: Joss should leave the real investigating to the professionals, like Liam. She's out of her depth.

Eileen1998: Wow, I didn't realize Joss was just a barista. No wonder her podcast is so amateur hour.

JusticeJunkie42: Are you even trying to find the real killer? What's the point?

I threw up my hands scaring Minnie from her sleep. The feline kept one eye on me as I complained. "I never said I was investigating. I mean sure, I'm curious, but I'm not stupid enough to hunt down a killer."

My phone beeped and I gladly swiped out of Instagram.

> **Andre:** You up?
>
> **Joss:** Yeah, just finishing up some work on the podcast. What's up?
>
> **Andre:** Rough day. I was hoping I could call you.
>
> **Joss:** Of course, you can always call me. Is everything okay?
>
> **Andre:** I just need to hear your voice. Give me a few minutes.
>
> **Joss:** I'll be here. Take your time.

I turned off the light on my nightstand and burrowed under the covers. Usually after we talked, I went to sleep pretty easily. Andre wouldn't admit it, but I think he liked doing the same. There were a few times I thought he did fall asleep on me but caught himself. I appreciated that despite being tired he still reached out.

A few minutes later, my phone rang, and I quickly answered, feeling a mix of concern and anticipation. "Hey there," I said softly.

"Hey, babe. How was your day?" Andre's voice sounded tired but warm.

I told him about my obsession with Liam's post and my conversation with Fay. "Did you and Detective Beckett find anything new in Rebecca's case?"

"No," Andre said, "but that was a good lead you had from Fay. When Rebecca disappeared, the detectives looked into Rebecca's computer and discovered that she was using a dating site called ArtisticConnections. They went through her matches and interactions, but none of the guys she hooked up with seemed to be viable suspects."

"She also lived in Savannah for a while."

Andre sighed. "That one may be a harder lead to follow. I can check to see if she reported anything to the police there."

I didn't want our entire conversation to be about the job, so I tried something more lighthearted. "I still need to find a dress for the gala. I thought about finding one online but Leesa talked me into going to some boutiques.

"I can't wait to see what you'll be wearing."

I grinned, remembering how incredible Andre had looked in his tuxedo at Leesa and Chris' wedding a few weeks ago. I teased. "I can't wait to see you in a tux again."

"I won't disappoint you." Andre chuckled softly. "You always know how to lift my spirits, Joss. Thanks for indulging me and letting me hear your voice. I should let you get some sleep."

Warmth spread through my chest. It was moments like these that reminded me how much I cared for him and how grateful I was to have him in my life, despite the challenges that came with dating a detective.

"You get some rest too, handsome."

I was about to return my phone to the nightstand when my phone's notification chime went off. I used to put my phone on do not disturb mode at night, but ever since I'd started dating Andre, I stopped doing that in case he needed to reach me.

I glanced at my phone, expecting it to be a direct message on Instagram. I had grown cautious about responding to DMs after an incident with a troll during my last podcast series. However, upon closer inspection, I realized it wasn't a DM but an actual text message.

Curious, I turned on the light on my nightstand to get a better look. The number seemed familiar, but I couldn't quite place it.

(848) 456-1324: I'm ready to talk.

A LATTE MAYHEM

My mind raced as I stared at the message trying to figure out who it could be and what they wanted to talk about. I sat up and grabbed my MacBook. I used to sleep with stuffed animals. Now I slept with electronics. I opened Google Docs, where I'd been keeping notes for the podcast and squinted at the list of contacts.

What?

The number belonged to Olivia Montgomery. Rebecca's sister was ready to talk.

The few times I had reached out to her in the past week, hoping to get an interview for my podcast, she'd never responded. Did seeing that video of her outburst plastered all over social media change her mind? Fay's warning to me and her thoughts about Olivia rushed into my mind.

What was Olivia ready to talk about? And why me?

Wednesday, June 26, 1:25 p.m.

I expected Olivia to invite me to her office. But the directions she sent were for a residential area. At first I thought maybe her office was in a house that had been converted for business purposes. As I entered the street, I realized this may have been where Oliva lived. A white BMW sat in the driveway. I pulled up behind it and looked up at the two story home. The grass must have been recently cut. There were grass trimmings along the driveway. Yellow and purple pansies were planted along the curve of the driveway leading up to the front door.

I rang the doorbell and waited. Yips sounded from inside. Olivia greeted me with a yapping Yorkie in her arms. She stared at me as if she wasn't sure why I was on her doorstep.

I cleared my throat. "Hi, I'm Joss Miller. We have an appointment for the interview."

"Joss," she stuttered. "Yes, come in."

"Thank you for inviting me."

Olivia stepped back. "Thank you for coming." The small dog yapped as I stepped inside.

Olivia soothed the dog. "Hush, Prince."

"What a cutie. And I'm sorry. There are three cats where I live, so he may smell cats on me."

Olivia smiled. "He will be fine. Let me put him in his playroom. I know you'll need some quiet so we can talk. Have a seat in the living room, I'll be right back."

A LATTE MAYHEM

I walked into a cozy living room. Somehow I expected it to be filled with modern furnishings and laminate wood floors. I could tell the wood floors were real and the couch and chairs were a bit older, but appeared well-maintained. I passed family photos of Olivia and Rebecca when they were younger. For the two women to not have been close, they appeared happy. In several photos, they were hugging each other or holding hands. There were also a few photos with a woman I assumed was the mother. Olivia looked more like their mother, but Rebecca shared their mom's complexion.

"I'm sorry to keep you waiting. Would you like anything?" Olivia showed up behind me.

I turned around. "No, I'm fine. Is this your mother?"

Olivia nodded. "Yes. She passed about five years ago. Breast cancer. Rebecca was her baby girl. In some ways, I'm glad our mother didn't have to experience Rebecca's disappearance."

"And how are you holding up?" I asked.

She looked at me. "As best I can. I appreciate you asking. Why don't we have a seat?"

I sat on the couch and Olivia sat across from me, her hands clasped tightly in her lap. "This was my mother's home. It was passed down to her by her mother. Rebecca and I grew up here."

"Oh, wow. It's a beautiful home."

Olivia rubbed her hands across the arms of the chair. "Where do we start? I've done a lot of interviews but never a podcast."

"Well, I'm honored. Before we start, can I ask why you wanted to talk to me? I mean I'm not a journalist. At least that's the word going around on social media."

Olivia's eyes hardened, her tone sharp. "We seemed to be getting harassed by the same, shall I say, shady individual." She glanced away as her features went slack. "I've been trying to get Vivian's attention for weeks. Maybe longer. When my sister first went missing, she seemed to want to help. Over the years, it seemed like she benefited off Rebecca's work at the gallery and she wouldn't take my calls. I know I made a fool out of myself on Sunday, but it was the only way I could get her attention. I wish I had thought about the fact that someone could have a camera and would put it on the Internet. I'm a lawyer, I should've known better."

"Can't you legally get him to take it down?"

Olivia shrugged. "It wouldn't do any good now. Once something gets out there on the Internet, it's out there forever."

I thought about all the other sites that had picked up the footage and knew Olivia was right.

She continued. "I listened to your episodes about your grandfather. It touched me that a young woman would want to dig into and expose the horrors of her family history. And the people who have been on your podcast in the past few weeks all spoke lovely things about Rebecca. I like what you're doing. You're reminding people that my sister was a beautiful individual who left us much too soon."

"I appreciate you taking the time to talk to me. If it's okay with you, I'll use my iPhone to record our interview." I pulled it out. "You requested I send your questions ahead of time. What were your thoughts?"

Olivia nodded and pulled a laptop toward her, then opened it. "These were fair questions. And I appreciate you sending them ahead of time so I could consider my responses."

Knowing that Olivia was a lawyer, I hoped she would really be genuine in her answers. This was pretty big for me considering she'd never been on a podcast before.

I pulled out my standard release form and handed it to her. I had a lawyer friend look over it last season, but I wasn't sure if Olivia would sign as she scrutinized every line of text.

"Do you have a pen? I would have to walk to my office."

I pulled a pen out of my bag and tried hard not to release my sigh of relief too loudly as she scribbled her signature.

When she handed me the paper, I noted the tremble in her hands.

I deliberately took my time putting the paper back in the manila folder. There was usually some unease when it came to doing an interview, but the tension in the air had goosebumps on my arms. I took a breath and reached for my phone.

She whipped out her hand suddenly to stop me. "Before you start recording, I want to say something off record."

As I sat across from Olivia, I couldn't help but notice the way her eyes lingered on my face. My discomfort grew by the second.

Was this the right thing to do? How many people told me not to do this interview?

"You know, Joss, it's uncanny how much you resemble Rebecca," Olivia said softly, a sad smile tugging at her lips. "When I first saw a photo of you, I did a double take."

I shifted in my seat, unsure how to respond. It wasn't the first time someone had commented on my resemblance to Rebecca, but coming from her sister, it felt particularly strange. Unsure how to respond, I didn't say anything.

Olivia didn't seem to mind. Her gaze became distant. When she finally took a deep breath, her eyes filled with tears. "Joss, I need to tell you something. Something that's been weighing on me ever since Rebecca disappeared."

I leaned forward, my doubts about this interview were making my stomach churn. "What is it, Olivia?"

"I let her down," Olivia whispered, her voice cracking with emotion. "I was supposed to be her big sister, her protector. But I was so caught up in my own life, my own problems, that I wasn't there for her when she needed me most."

Tears spilled down Olivia's cheeks, and I felt my own eyes growing damp. "Olivia, you can't blame yourself. You couldn't have known what was going to happen."

She shook her head, a bitter laugh escaping her lips. "But that's just it, Joss. I should have known. My mother told me to take care of my younger sister. We barely even talked to each other."

"I've seen you, Olivia. You have been relentless about seeing her found and you will find justice for her."

She took a shuddering breath before she met my eyes. "I need to do what I couldn't do for her when she was alive."

I smiled softly. "I have some women in my life who would tell me this is a good time to pray. Would you like to do that before we begin?"

Olivia smiled. "Yes, I very much would like to do that."

"Let's pray."

Chapter 12
Chaos

COLD JUSTICE PODCAST

Season 2, Episode 4: A Sister's Confession
Published: June 27

Joss: Welcome back to another episode of the *Cold Justice* Podcast. This season we're talking to people who knew Rebecca Montgomery. The police are continuing to find leads on what happened to her when she disappeared three years ago. Today, we'll be diving deeper into Rebecca's story by speaking with someone who knew her better than anyone else - her sister, Olivia.

Olivia Montgomery is a successful lawyer who has been tirelessly searching for answers about her sister's disappearance. Despite the emotional toll it has taken on her, Olivia has never given up hope of finding out what happened to Rebecca.

In this exclusive interview, Olivia will be sharing her memories of Rebecca, their childhood together, and the events leading up to her sister's disappearance. She'll also be revealing some new information that she's never before shared publicly—information that could potentially shed new light on the case.

This is the *Cold Justice* Podcast. Let's get into it!

Joss: Olivia, thank you so much for agreeing to speak with me today. I know how difficult this must be for you, and I appreciate your willingness to talk about your sister with our listeners.

Olivia: Thank you for having me, Joss. It's not easy to talk about what happened to Rebecca, but I feel like it's important to keep her story alive. I'm hoping that by speaking out, I can get some closure about what happened to her. Somebody out there knows.

Joss: I agree. Someone knows something. Olivia, why don't you tell us a little about your relationship with Rebecca? What was it like growing up together?

Olivia: Rebecca was always a free spirit, even as a child. She saw the world in a different way than I did. I guess some siblings grow apart as they get older. While I was focused on my studies and building a career, Rebecca was busy chasing her next creative endeavor. We didn't always see eye to eye, but I felt protective of her, even when she didn't want me to be. She was my baby sister.

Joss: And what about Rebecca's love for art? When did that passion develop?

Olivia: Oh my goodness! From the moment she could hold a crayon (laughs), Rebecca was always creating something. I should have known she would paint murals. I remember one time she got in trouble for making a rainbow on the wall of her bedroom. Our mother was mad about it at first, but then I guess it was too much trouble to clean or paint over. I think our mother knew Rebecca had this innate need to express herself through her artwork. As she grew older, that passion only intensified.

Joss: Olivia, I know this is difficult, but do you have any thoughts on what might have happened to Rebecca?

Olivia: Joss, I wish I knew. I know someone out there hurt Rebecca. Someone that she knew.

Joss: Why do you think it was someone she knew?

Olivia: This is something that I haven't admitted to anyone before, Joss. I'm not sure why I'm sharing it with you.

Joss: Are you sure you want to do that? You know I will publish this podcast.

Olivia: (remains quiet for a few seconds) Yes (takes a deep breath). Maybe it will help someone else come forward. The police have never been able to find any leads.

(shaky voice) The night before Rebecca disappeared, she called me. It was late, and I could tell something was wrong. She was rambling, saying things that didn't make sense. She mentioned someone had been bothering her and that she might need to leave Charleston.

Joss: Oh my! She wanted to leave Charleston? Did she give you any details about a person or her plans?

Olivia: No, she didn't. If I'm honest, I assumed she was having some type of mental breakdown. It wasn't the first time.

Joss: Oh! She'd had some mental issues before?

Olivia: (sighs) Off and on. Rebecca was really sensitive. Our mother called her our Alice in Wonderland because she wasn't always focused in reality.

A LATTE MAYHEM

Joss: Why did you think Claude McKnight had something to do with Rebecca's disappearance? Didn't you all grow up together?

Olivia: (silence) Yes, I was ahead of them in school. Claude and Rebecca had always been an inseparable pair. More like brother and sister. Well, at least that's the way Rebecca thought of him. Truthfully, I don't know why I focused on Claude.

I guess after Rebecca called me, I was worried about her. It'd been awhile since we'd gotten together. I went to the gala that Saturday before, but she had so many people around her. So when I showed up to Rebecca's apartment the next day, I wanted to tell her how much I loved the mural she'd painted at the gallery. It was beautiful. I was so proud of her. Our mother would have been proud of her too. I wanted to understand why she wanted to leave Charleston. She had accomplished so much.

Before I pressed the doorbell, I heard her arguing with someone. I'd been standing there trying to hear (laughs). Eavesdropping, I know. But I was concerned. Then Claude opened the front door in a huff. He looked so angry, I just moved out of his way as he rushed by me. I could see Rebecca was upset. I asked her if he'd hurt her. She told me no, but I could tell she was agitated and scared. I'd never seen her like that before. I tried to get her to talk to me, but she wanted me to go. She said she would be alright and not to worry. So I left.

It wasn't until I heard your interview with Claude that I realized he knew something was wrong too. He wanted to help her and he was frustrated that she didn't trust him.

Joss: That's right. Let's go back. You said she called you the night before she disappeared. What was she saying?

Olivia: (voice shaking) I didn't … actually talk to her. She left that message on my voicemail. The police know about it, of course. Like I said, they never figured out who would make Rebecca scared or what would drive her away from her home. She'd just revealed one of her most successful murals and I'm sure she had many other jobs coming her way.

(sob) It didn't make any sense. I tried calling her back the next morning, but she didn't answer. I felt like she needed to see someone. A professional. I called over and over that day. When I couldn't reach her, I knew something terrible had happened. I just knew it. So I went to the police, but there wasn't much they could do. She was an adult.

I wish I had been closer to my sister so she would have confided in me. I know she reached out to me for help. That wasn't like her. I should have not left that day and insisted she talk.

A LATTE MAYHEM

Joss: Olivia, I'm so sorry you've had to carry this with you for so long. It sounds like it's possible your sister was scared of someone and they could have been responsible for her disappearance (pause). On the first episode, Claude felt the same way. Are you sure there wasn't someone in Rebecca's life that would have harmed her? Is it possible one of her past boyfriends was bothering her?

Olivia: (silent) Rebecca was involved with someone. A prominent businessman. He was supportive after Rebecca's disappearance, checking in with me to see how I was doing. We haven't touched base in over a year. I've heard that he's moved on. Not that I blame him.

I have wondered if my sister was under some type of duress in that relationship. Rebecca was fiery and passionate, and sometimes she attracted the wrong kind of men. Like I said, she was sensitive. She took things to heart and she had some great loves in her short life.

Joss: I understand she attended and also spent time teaching at SCAD, the Savannah College of Art and Design. Do you know anything about her life there?

Olivia: No, but I really didn't stay in touch with my sister while she was in Savannah. She only came home during the holidays, so I'm afraid we were even more apart. While she was in school, I was in law school and then studying for the bar.

Joss: I see. Well, Olivia, thank you for spending time with me and my listeners. I know it wasn't easy. Is there anything else you'd like to add?

Olivia: Just that I won't stop searching for the truth. Rebecca deserves justice, and I won't rest until I find out what happened to her that night. I owe it to her and my mother. At least they are together now. I know that both of them are in heaven.

Joss: Olivia, thank you again for your bravery and for trusting me with your story. If anyone out there knows something, please come forward.

This is Joss with *Cold Justice* podcast.

Friday, June 28, 10:14 a.m.

I barely slept and decided to get up for work after maybe three hours of sleep. Though I felt like a whiz with the new editing software, for the first time I wondered how much I should cut from the interview. Olivia's startling confession haunted me. No wonder the woman felt guilty. And Rebecca was obviously under some mental stress, but it had to be because of someone.

I really had doubts about publishing the episode, but I launched episode four live after midnight. Out of all the interviews, even Claude's, I didn't expect that kind of vulnerability. In the end, I kept most of the interview. I hoped some listener's memory would be stirred to help the police. Andre told me the tip hotline hadn't sprung any leads.

We never stated Ethan Turner's name, but it wouldn't take long for anyone who followed the case to know who Olivia alluded to. She slipped her suspicions without stating his name. She was a lawyer, so while she may have revealed some things, she also kept her answers safe.

I had a tiny bit of anxiety about releasing this episode without sharing it with Andre. I wasn't sure what he'd think of the episode. Olivia said she'd told the police what she told me, and Andre admitted the former detectives focused too long on Claude. But knowing Rebecca wanted to pack her bags and leave Charleston, that would have made them not take her disappearance quite as seriously either.

What puzzled me the most, I couldn't understand why Rebecca wouldn't talk to anyone. Everyone I'd interviewed or had a conversation with had noticed that something was off about her. But most admitted that Rebecca pushed them away.

How can you help someone who needs help, but doesn't want it?

I thought about a friend from college who seemed like the happiest person in the world. She'd been a cheerleader all through high school and in college. But one day she could no longer hide under a smile and makeup. Her boyfriend went on a rampage that landed her in the hospital. On the outside, he seemed like the nicest guy and they were such a good looking couple.

I'd had some scary run-ins with guys with tempers too. Was this that? If so, I could see Rebecca being ashamed and ready to get away.

From what I could gather, Rebecca and Ethan had been a couple for over a year. What did he know about her? Or was he the problem?

Someone as wealthy and influential as Ethan could have made it hard for Rebecca to say anything. That's probably what Andre and his partner thought. The man I briefly glimpsed at Magnolia Media appeared to be a mogul on a mission. But who was he behind closed doors?

After the mid-morning rush at the café, I took a breather in the back and pulled out my phone. To my surprise, episode four had the most downloads ever. Olivia's revelation that her sister had reached out the night before she disappeared with thoughts of leaving Charleston had people buzzing on social media. I read through comments that blatantly pointed to Ethan, many curious about his involvement.

Fay walked by. "This morning's episode has people stirred up, I see."

I looked up. "Did you listen to it yet?"

Fay pulled out a tray of fresh banana nut muffins. "I heard it while I was baking this morning. I meant to say something to you, but once the doors opened, we were so busy. Girl, you must have a way of getting people to talk to you. I can't believe Olivia was so candid with you. That didn't seem like her at all."

"I was surprised too. And I had some doubts about what to cut from the interview. All of it seemed important. Fay, did you know Rebecca wanted to leave Charleston?"

Fay shook her head. "No, but you know we hadn't talked to each other in a while. I may or may not have mentioned this, but when she started dating Ethan, we didn't hang out as much. Sometimes she stopped by the café. Like you, she loved the vanilla latte. But we only spoke in passing the last few months before she disappeared."

I frowned. "Claude said that too."

Fay asked, "So has your man said anything about the episode? He hasn't been stopping by the café in the morning. He's not getting his coffee someplace else is he?"

"Only the police station. He's really busy... slammed with a lot of cases." I shut my mouth and then blew out a breath. Then I confessed. "He's not saying it, but doing this podcast may not have been the best choice. He's trying to be supportive and I... didn't tell him I interviewed Olivia."

Fay's eyes opened wide. "Oh, Joss. Don't mess up your relationship over this."

"That's not my intention. Things happened so fast and I just didn't have time to tell him."

Fay folded her arms and looked at me over her glasses.

"I know, I know. It's too late now. He's probably heard it." I held up my phone. "This has been my most downloaded episode."

My phone rang, and I turned it around to look at the screen. "Oh no."

"What's wrong?"

I looked at Fay. "It's Olivia. Do you mind if I take this really quick? I know I need to get back up front."

"I got it." Fay pointed. "You better see what she wants. I told you she could be trouble for you."

A LATTE MAYHEM

A feeling of unease settled over me. "Hello, this is Joss."

"Joss, I need you to take down the episode." Olivia's voice was tight with anxiety.

"What? Why?" I asked, surprised by her sudden change of heart.

"I just heard from Ethan's lawyer. I didn't even say the man's name, but he's accusing me of slander. You need to watch your back too. If he hasn't already contacted you, he will."

"But there is such a thing as free speech. And his name was never mentioned."

Olivia sighed. "He's a narcissist. And according to him, everyone in the world knows he and Rebecca were a couple before she disappeared. Just know, if you don't take the episode down, you will hear from him. I'm starting to wonder about him even more. He's too busy worrying about his reputation than the fact that somebody murdered my sister. I've got to go."

I hung up the phone, my mind racing. I wasn't going to take down the episode. It would undermine the integrity of the podcast and I still had Liam's shady trolls all in my comments. If I took the episode down, the level of cattiness would be unbearable. Plus, it was out there, on the internet.

Was I as bad as Liam posting that footage from his phone camera?

No, I wasn't. Olivia was a grown woman and a lawyer. She knew exactly what she said and she signed a release form.

I rubbed my eyes, feeling the weight of everything bearing down on me. It was almost lunch hour and I had to get back to work.

If Ethan Turner had something to hide, maybe he needed to sweat a little about it. That episode would keep getting downloads.

Friday, June 28, 5:55 p.m.

While I wiped down tables, Eleanor gathered up her laptop. I'd told her what happened, and she, like many others, had already listened to Olivia's interview.

"Joss, you can't take down that episode," Eleanor said, her brow furrowed with concern. "Olivia knew what she was saying would cause controversy. Just like when she showed up at Vivian's tea party and started a commotion."

I sighed. "I know. But I also don't want any beef from Ethan Turner either."

Eleanor pulled her laptop satchel over her shoulders. "Well, give him an opportunity to say his piece."

I started to say Andre didn't want me to approach the man, but then I paused. "Do you think that would help? Giving him a chance to tell his side of the story on the podcast. Kind of the way Claude was able to for the first episode."

Eleanor bobbed her head up and down. "Exactly. He has to be the next one you interview. It makes perfect sense. You have a good night, dear. Don't let anyone intimidate you."

"Thanks, Eleanor." I walked her to the door and closed it behind her. With the sign turned to closed, I switched off the lights and headed into the back.

Fay looked up from her office chair as I entered. "Did Eleanor leave?"

"Yes. She thinks I should reach out and offer to interview Ethan."

Fay raised an eyebrow. "Is that wise?"

"Well, it might keep me from destroying this season of the podcast. I'm no journalist, but it seems fair to interview all parties involved and let them have their say."

Fay spun her chair around to face me. "But suppose Ethan really did have something to do with Rebecca's disappearance?"

I shrugged. "I wouldn't be the first person to make that suggestion. It's all over social media."

Fay started to say something but suddenly a loud shattering sound echoed through the café. Fay and I looked at each other, eyes wide with alarm.

Fay jumped up. "What in the world?" She rushed toward the front of the café with me right behind her.

She stopped to flip the lights back on in the dining area.

We both sucked in a breath.

The window next to the door's entrance had been smashed. Shards of glass littered the floor. Outside the window, two figures with hoods were running away.

Fay let loose a stream of expletives and started toward the door.

I shouted. "Fay, be careful. There is glass everywhere."

Fay skidded her tracks, her face a mass of anger. "This has to be Rick Nelson and those developers trying to intimidate me into selling the café. I can't believe they would sink this low."

I knew other owners on the block were complaining, but I'd never heard about vandalism claims. "I'll call the police." I had my phone already in hand, so I dialed 911. While I relayed the address and told the dispatcher about the damage, Fay paced. Her anger turned to tears, which ran down her face.

A LATTE MAYHEM

"The police will be here soon. Let's sit down and wait for them."

I guided Fay away from the window to a table near the counter. With the sounds of cars passing by through the broken window, it felt like our cozy café was open to the world and not safe anymore. I wasn't sure Fay saw it, but underneath a table, I caught sight of a brick. They must have launched it through the window. The police would need to deal with that. I hoped it had some fingerprints. We could only hope for someone to be so brazen that their stupidity would lead to them getting caught.

Fay wiped her face. "I'm so mad. Oh my goodness, I need to call Joe. He's cooking dinner tonight and I'm going to be late."

I nodded. "Maybe you should tell him to come here. We can't leave that window like that tonight. I will stay as long as you need me."

While Fay dialed Joe, my phone buzzed with a notification. With a quick glance at my locked screen, I noticed it was from Instagram. I'd turned off all other notifications from posts and comments. But in case someone wanted to reach me through my DMs, I kept those notifications on.

It was from a user I didn't recognize. They followed me, but I didn't follow them. Out of curiosity, I clicked on the message.

A chill crawled up my spine.

Watcher_98: Back off the Montgomery case, or you'll be sorry.

Watcher? That's creepy!

I noted the timing. It was sent a few minutes ago. I wondered if the broken window was indeed a tactic employed by Rick Nelson or if someone was trying to send me a message. I didn't want to show it to Fay since she was already upset. I needed to think.

My podcast audience knew I was a barista by day, but I couldn't imagine why someone would take their concerns with me out on the café. There were two figures running away from the café. Teenagers or young people by the appearance of the hoodies and the way they ran.

Fay had a camera in the corner of the shop that showed anyone who entered the café and a camera on the back door. Those were put in when I first started working here. "Fay, are there any nearby cameras that face the café?"

Fay rubbed her arms. "There might be cameras across the street at the furniture store. I'm not sure who else has cameras on this block. Didn't it look like kids running down the street? And what did they hit the window with?" She stood up to look at the floor. Then she screeched, "Is that a brick?"

A LATTE MAYHEM

"Don't touch it. Maybe the police can get fingerprints." We already knew the person who threw the brick lacked sense. It's possible they hadn't worn gloves.

Sirens drew close and soon a police cruiser pulled up in front of the café. The sight of the police reminded me of last fall when I sat waiting for them after stumbling upon a body next door.

Fay rushed over to the door to meet the officers. As she recounted what happened, I noticed another car roll up behind the police car.

Recognizing the figure that stepped out, my heart sank.

Andre and his partner.

I wanted to run and hide, but it was too late. Andre walked up to the broken window, and his eyes met mine through the shattered glass.

Despite the vandalism, I had a sinking feeling he would want to talk to me about something else. Why else would two homicide detectives show up?

Chapter 13

Getting Too Hot

Friday, June 28, 6:40 p.m.

No one else died. That was good! Andre and Detective Beckett approached me while Fay chatted with the deputies.

When he reached me, Andre stroked my arm. "Are you okay?"

I nodded. "I'm fine. I just hate this happened. We were in the back closing up the café for the night. It looked like two teenagers that ran off, but I can't be sure. They had on hoodies, which is nuts because it's like ninety degrees out there."

Andre glanced around. "Can we sit for a minute? First, let me introduce you to my partner. Beckett, this is Joss Miller."

"Nice to finally meet you, Joss. You've been creating quite a stir with your podcast." Detective Beckett stared at me with icy gray eyes. Despite the lightness of his eyes, he had a friendly face. Unlike most men his age, with the exception of the paunch poking out from underneath his suit jacket, he'd maintained a decent physique. He and Andre both had a few days of scruff on their faces and looked equally tired.

"That wasn't my intention. I promise. We can sit in the booth over there."

The booth was Eleanor's usual spot. She would be as upset about the broken window as us, but would also be delighted that cops had used her booth to talk business.

I slid into the booth and Andre scooted in beside me. With a few grunts, Detective Beckett climbed in across from us.

"I'm sorry. I should have asked if you wanted some coffee. I don't think Fay would mind if I made a fresh batch."

Detective Beckett shook his head. "No, that's fine. Baez here will tell you I've had enough coffee for the day. I'm already going to be up tonight."

Andre glanced at me, his eyes solemn. "Joss, we need to talk about Olivia's interview. It's raised some concerns for us."

"What kind of concerns?"

Beckett chimed in, "We're worried that the information Olivia shared could potentially hinder the investigation."

I furrowed my brow. "You mean this would upset Ethan Turner."

Detective Beckett glanced at Andre and then eyed me. "Why would you say that?"

Andre sighed and purposely didn't look at me. "Did he reach out to you?"

"No, but Olivia called me. She wanted me to pull the episode even though she consented to it. It wasn't like she outright accused him, but he'd apparently reached out to her and threatened to sue her."

Andre looked at me. "Really. So what are you going to do?"

I shrugged. "I can't pull it down now. Besides, if an interview that didn't even mention Ethan's name upset him, maybe he is guilty of something."

Beckett clasped his hands together. "Joss has some points there. Ethan was close to Rebecca, and we know they had some issues in their relationship. It's possible that he knew more about her disappearance than he initially let on."

I touched Andre's hand, I already knew he would be upset. "I think I should interview Ethan. I know, I know. You said not to, but I should give him an opportunity to share his side of the story. Suppose he does like Olivia and feels comfortable enough to say more than he's told you all."

Andre's tone was clipped. "I told you it could be dangerous."

Beckett, who had been listening intently, interjected. "Now hold on a minute, Baez. Joss is a smart girl and it's apparent she's got a knack for getting people to open up. Ethan might slip up and say something."

I looked at Andre. "If there's a chance Ethan knows something, I can talk to him. Besides, I think people are going to be expecting me to interview him at this point."

Andre ran a hand over his head, clearly frustrated. "I don't like it, Joss."

Beckett suggested. "We can be nearby in case anything goes wrong."

I smiled, grateful for the older detective's support. "With you and Beckett watching my back, I feel more confident about meeting with Ethan."

Beckett grinned. "Sounds like a plan. I'm going over to talk to the deputies, see what's next for figuring out what happened here. You all will need to get that window boarded up."

I glanced over at the counter and saw Joe had arrived while we'd been talking. He had his arm around Fay. "Joe is a plumber but also an excellent handyman. I know he will get it fixed for her."

A LATTE MAYHEM

After Beckett walked away, I peered at Andre. "There's something I need to show you. I only wanted you to see it because I'm not sure what to make of it."

"What is it?" He leaned forward, our shoulders touching. The warmth of his body made me feel even more protected inside the booth. I pulled up the direct message on Instagram. "It may be nothing, but a few minutes after someone threw ... the brick through the window, I received this."

Andre studied the message but didn't say anything.

I gulped. "It could be totally unrelated."

He turned, his gaze focused on my face. We were so close, we could have kissed, but that would have been entirely inappropriate. Instead, Andre stated, "This could be a coincidence. But this is also the kind of thing I wanted you to not have to deal with. It's bad enough that Liam dude has focused his followers on you. People get uptight and focus on the craziest stuff."

"I get it. I don't have to interview Ethan. I just want to make sure he doesn't want to sue me too. Not that there's much he's going to get from my poor bank account."

Andre shook his head. "Do it. Let me know when you set things up with Ethan."

"Suppose he doesn't want to talk to me."

Andre rubbed at the scruff on his face. "He's going to want to talk to you. Ethan doesn't ignore pretty women."

I wasn't sure if I should have been offended or if Andre was making a point.

Either way, I started typing an inquiry to submit to Ethan's email address.

Friday, June 28, 10:32 p.m.

By the time I arrived home, it was late. My grandmother had left me a note on the kitchen table, but I was too tired to heat up any of the spinach quiche she made. Instead, I opted for a bowl of Honey Nut Cheerios and headed up to bed.

I felt compelled to let Oliva know about my decision. I set my cereal bowl on the desk and flipped open my laptop. Behind me, the tuxedo cat had already made herself comfortable on my bed. She stretched and yawned, then curled back up to sleep.

"I'm glad one of us is having a peaceful night."

I quickly typed out a message to Olivia, my fingers flying over the keyboard.

Subject: Cold Justice Podcast – Episode Request
Hey Olivia,

I decided not to take down the episode since it's already sparked so much interest and conversation. I do want you to know I will be reaching out to Ethan. I've been encouraged to give him an opportunity to talk.

All the best,

Joss

I hit send, hoping Olivia would understand my decision and the importance of keeping the episode up. While I waited to see if she would respond, I pulled up the list of questions I'd prepared for my interview with her.

That's when it hit me. There was still a glaring hole in Rebecca's history, a period of time that I knew almost nothing about. Her years in Savannah. Fay thought Rebecca might have dated someone there. Rebecca taught at the art school, and I had a connection.

It was late, but I felt like I would get a text back pretty quickly.

Nyla B lived on her texts. And her older sister was the person I needed to contact. A talented photographer, Simone Masters not only had her photos featured in magazines and museums across the United States, she also was a professor.

> **Joss:** What's up, Nyla? Quick question. Is Simone still at SCAD?
>
> **Nyla B:** Hey, girl! Yeah, she's still there. You looking to go back to school now?
>
> **Joss:** LOL. No, I wanted to see if she remembers Rebecca Montgomery from when she taught there.
>
> **Nyla B:** Look at you, Ms. Investigator. I will send you her email. She's not a night owl like us.
>
> **Joss:** Thanks, Nyla. You're the best.

As promised, the email address came right away. I quickly opened up my email and drafted a message to Simone.

Subject: Rebecca Montgomery - Cold Justice Podcast

Hey Simone,

I hope this email finds you well. It's been a while.

I'm reaching out because I'm doing some research. Your sister, Nyla B, may have told you about my podcast. She's been a huge help to me. This season I've been investigating the disappearance of Rebecca Montgomery.

I recently learned she attended and later taught at the Savannah College of Art and Design. I was wondering if you might have known Rebecca during her time there. You know, sometimes it's a small world.

If you have any information about Rebecca's time in Savannah, no matter how small or seemingly insignificant, I would appreciate it if you can let me know. Even if you didn't know her personally, maybe you heard something through mutual friends or the local art scene.

I'm including a link to the podcast below. If you have a chance, I'd really appreciate it if you could give it a listen and let me know your thoughts.

Thank you so much for your time and consideration, Simone. I hope to hear back from you soon, but no pressure at all.

All the best,

Joss

My eyes were starting to seriously droop and my body longed for the bed. By the time I freshened up and changed into one of

Andre's t-shirts I had snagged, I was ready to conk out for the night.

But as soon as my head hit the pillow, I couldn't shake the feeling that Andre might be upset with me about my decision to interview Ethan. Wearing his shirt probably triggered me. I picked up my phone and called him, hoping to clear the air so I could sleep.

His phone rang and rang. Then I realized he might be sleeping.

"Hello," he answered, sounding groggy.

I grimaced. "I'm sorry. I woke you up."

"It's fine. What's wrong? Did you get another weird message?"

"No, and I didn't check either. I needed to know if me and you are okay."

Andre sighed. "I'm not upset, Joss. I'm worried about you. But we will work out a plan if Ethan decides to talk to you."

A wave of relief washed over me. "That means a lot to me. There's a chance he might not even want to talk."

Andre replied. "But if he does, we'll handle it together. Understood."

"Absolutely." I hesitated for a moment, wondering if I should tell him that I reached out to Nyla B's sister about

Rebecca's time in Savannah. No, I'd stirred enough hornet's nests with me and Andre. I would wait until I heard back from Simone. Besides, it was enough to have to deal with Ethan Turner. I could be barking up the wrong tree with the Savannah angle. And I wasn't investigating.

Just curious!

"Goodnight, Andre. " I said, smiling into the phone.

"Goodnight, Joss. Sweet dreams," he replied before ending the call.

This time when I laid my head back on the pillow, the cat nestled next to me. The purrs of the cat lulled me into a deep sleep.

I was pretty sure Andre showed up in my dreams too. He usually did.

Saturday, June 29, 7:45 a.m.

I arrived at the café early the next morning ready to help with the cleanup efforts. To my surprise, Fay and Joe had already swept up the glass and boarded up the window. It was definitely a different look, but everything inside the café appeared normal and in place. I headed to the back. Fay was preparing the café for opening.

"Joe fixed up the window pretty good."

Fay glanced up as I approached. She looked like she hadn't slept at all. "Yes. I complain about the costs, but I'm grateful I have insurance. I'm still coming out from under the car repairs. And on top of that, something is wrong with the camera over the back door."

I placed my bag in my locker and grabbed my apron. "Did the cops say what happens next?" Then I stopped as my mind caught up to what Fay had said. "Wait, the back door camera isn't working?"

She sighed. "The cops wanted to look at all the cameras, but something's wrong with the one over the back door. Not that it matters. We usually only open the back door for deliveries and taking out the trash. I added the camera back there more for checking out who's at the back door."

"Anyway, the cops are going to see if the other shop owners have any camera footage. The back door camera will get fixed after I get the window replaced. I told them about Rick Nelson intimidating some of the other shop owners. Of course, they told me that I had no proof." She grimaced. "They're right, but

I have a strong feeling he may use other tactics to get us to move from this location for his development project."

I really hoped the vandalism wasn't as sinister as I imagined. I didn't know if I should tell Fay that it could have had something to do with my podcast. But I wasn't really sure. And I wasn't trying to get fired, not that she would do that to me.

As the morning progressed, word about the vandalism spread to other shop owners and people who normally visited the café. It felt like a larger than normal crowd. Many of our regular customers showed their support, offering kind words and encouragement.

Even Liam made an appearance. "It's a shame that someone would do that. How are you doing, Joss? You are blowing it out of the water with those interviews. Any thoughts to who's next?"

I smiled at him sweetly. "Thank you for listening. I didn't think you were impressed with the barista producing a true crime podcast."

Liam attempted to blush. "I'm sorry about that. You know I have to please my followers and sponsors by bringing in the traffic."

"Seems like a really hard way to make a living. What can I get you?"

He grinned. "Just a black coffee."

I gladly poured his coffee and looked forward to him leaving. He wasn't a bad guy if he wasn't so interested in getting paid for attention. Still I wished Fay could really ban people like him from the café.

After I handed him his coffee, to my dismay, Liam didn't leave. He found a seat by the window and took out his laptop. I soon forgot about him as customers continued to trickle in.

I wasn't sure if it was Fay or one of the other baristas, but a jar had been set up on the counter for donations and it was filling up pretty fast. Eleanor came up to the counter after the morning crowd had died down some. She placed her own donation in the jar and stated. "It's a shame someone would do this to our favorite place. Are there any leads on who did this?"

I shook my head. "Nope." Then I turned around to look behind me. "Do you have a minute? I want to run something by you."

"Absolutely. By the way, I could use a refill." Eleanor winked.

I smiled and grabbed the carafe. I figured if anyone could help me figure out the message I received and the timing of the broken window, our resident mystery author could provide insight.

A LATTE MAYHEM

I pulled out my phone and showed the message to Eleanor. While she read, I refilled her cup and told her about the timeline. "What do you think?"

Eleanor kept her voice low. "I think you are having a time with this podcast. Between your exclusive interviews and the trolls online."

I rolled my eyes. "The trolls are thanks to a disgruntled wanna be reporter who happens to have a following." I looked behind Eleanor and saw that Liam must have finally left.

Eleanor chuckled, but then grew serious. "This watcher person, if I had to plot this out in a novel, this person may know exactly what happened to Rebecca."

I was on the clock, but I had to sit. "That's what's been in the back of my mind."

Eleanor asked, "Does your detective know about this?"

I nodded. "Yeah, I showed Andre last night. It made him feel uneasy too. His partner Detective Beckett also agreed with you about reaching out to Ethan." I frowned. "I wondered if Ethan could have created this watcher profile, but something about that didn't strike me as plausible. I don't really know him, but it doesn't seem like something he would do."

Eleanor took a sip of her freshened coffee. "No, the watcher profile is someone who likes to hide behind social media. I agree that Ethan would come to you directly."

"Like the way he reached out to Olivia, letting her know he would sue her. You know he still hasn't said anything to me. He didn't ask me to take down the episode either."

Eleanor tilted her head. "Maybe he's expecting you to ask him for an interview."

I thought back to my first and only encounter with Ethan when I visited Magnolia Media a few weeks ago. He knew who I was after I told him I was a podcaster.

"Oh no!" Eleanor murmured.

"What?" I turned around half-expecting to see Ethan Turner.

But it wasn't him.

Fireworks were about to start though as Fay stepped out from the back.

Rick Nelson himself made a surprise appearance in the café. The first thing he did was turn to look at the boarded up window.

Maybe he really was behind the vandalism.

"May I help you, Mr. Nelson?" Fay stood behind the counter with a stony expression.

In case Fay got a bit riled up, I quickly moved behind the counter and replaced the carafe. I would either have to hold my boss back or jump in with her.

Rick walked toward the counter pointing at the boarded up window. "Oh my! This used to be such a safe neighborhood. My sister's death last fall created a hole in my family. Now this repeated vandalism is starting to be a problem."

Had other shop owners been experiencing this too?

Fay held her ground. "Most of us have been around for years and have never experienced these kinds of issues. Almost feels like someone is doing it on purpose."

Rick offered a stiff smile. "I'm really sorry this has happened to your café. I will do what I can to ensure anyone involved is found and punished. In the meantime, I would love a cup of black coffee and one of those banana nut muffins."

I stepped forward to pull out a muffin. Fay and I exchanged skeptical glances, then she poured the coffee and personally rang up the order.

"Thank you for the great service." Rick bit into the muffin. "Mmm, good. You all have a good day. Let me know if I can help you out."

As soon as Rick left the café, Fay slapped the counter. "He has some nerve to come in here gloating. I'm telling you that man is responsible for what happened last night."

Now that the man had shown up in person, I no longer doubted it. Rick was a wealthy businessman who made no secret of his desire to get his way, no matter the cost. I couldn't help but wonder how much Ethan Turner could be like him.

Both were powerful men used to getting what they wanted.

Did Ethan want something from Rebecca that she didn't want to give him? Did she lose her life in the process?

Chapter 14
The Mogul Boyfriend

Monday, July 1, 9:18 a.m.

This time of year, Fay took on an extra college student who could use the extra hours, but I still hated not being at the café. The tourist season had picked up and with the window still boarded up, I knew Fay was trying to make the best of things.

I called Fay on Sunday evening to request Monday off, and she'd told me, "Do what you need to do. You really have a knack for getting people to open up to you. I'm still having trouble feeling sorry for Olivia even though she lost a sister. I'm telling you she was horrible to Becca."

"I believe you, but she's given the best clues so far. I believe something happened to Rebecca for her to go to the last person you would expect – her estranged sister."

Fay made a soft 'hmm' sound. "It is weird. Maybe when you speak with Ethan Turner, he'll confess to you."

"I don't know how much he will tell me. He was pretty closed mouth with the police. Anyway, I sent him some suggested interview questions earlier. Guests can select to not respond."

"Let's hope something else profound comes from the interview."

I hoped for the same thing as I rose early Monday morning to battle traffic. Once I stepped through the glass doors of Synaptic, my eyes were immediately drawn to the stunning mural Rebecca had painted. The artwork was a mesmerizing blend of vibrant colors and abstract shapes with intricate patterns that seemed to pulse with energy. At the center of the mural, a humanoid figure emerged from a sea of binary code. Its eyes glowed with an otherworldly light.

She was so talented.

In her short life, Rebecca had left quite a legacy with her massive creations.

A voice from my left pulled me out of my thoughts. "Can I help you?"

So entranced with the mural, I didn't register the man behind the dark wooden desk. I expected a receptionist in the lobby, not a security guard. But then I remembered this was a tech company. Studying the lobby a little more, I wondered how strict they were about letting people inside the building. I was pretty sure I would be led to an office area and not in the part of the building where the magic happened.

As I approached the desk, the man eyed me. My nervousness returned and I clutched my bag in front of me. True to his word, Andre insisted I place an AirTag in my bag. Beckett wanted me to wear a wire, but I told them whatever I recorded had to have permission from Ethan, and they could listen to my raw files. I had a tendency to use most of my recordings so the public would hear the same thing, albeit more edited and polished.

"I'm Joss Miller. I have an appointment with Ethan Turner."

The security guard tapped a few keys on his computer and then scrutinized me more closely. "Ms. Miller. Do you have ID?"

A familiar voice said, "No need to do that, Steven. I will walk Joss back."

Startled, I turned to see Miranda approaching the guard's desk. Today, her blond hair hung around her shoulders.

Still looking suspicious, the guard grunted, "Ms. Blackwell, it's good to see you."

"You as well." She beamed at the guard before turning toward me. "Good morning, Joss."

"Hello, Miranda. It's good to see you again. Are you in this interview too?"

She laughed lightly. "Oh no. As Ethan's publicist, I came to make sure he behaved himself."

Behaved himself? Was his lawyer going to be here too?

I must have had a peculiar look on my face when Miranda glanced at me. She stopped. "I'm sorry. That came out wrong. I'll be direct, Joss. It's been a difficult time for Ethan with Rebecca's remains being found, harassment from the police and then Olivia making claims that Ethan could have had something to do with her sister's disappearance."

I met her gaze. "But Olivia didn't mention his name."

Miranda pursed her lips. "It was inferred. And people knew about their relationship. It's not fair."

I bit my lip. "It wasn't fair to Claude McKnight either when he was accused of having something to do with Rebecca's disappearance. Look, I've already interviewed you. Did you get any sense that I would be unfair?"

Miranda pouted. "Of course not, but Ethan has a lot more at stake. His company is revealing their next product in a few weeks. The gala coming up next weekend is also very high profile."

I held up a hand. "Let me be clear. Ethan can trust me. If he doesn't want to do this interview, I can turn around and leave. Besides, I could have mentioned on my podcast that you and Ethan are in a relationship. But that's not my style and I respect you both."

Miranda stiffened almost imperceptibly before regaining her composure. "I see. I will take you to Ethan's office." She turned briskly and I kept up until we stopped in front of a glass-walled room with a view of the city skyline. Ethan sat behind a long desk on the phone. His eyes locked on mine as I entered his office, a small smile played on his lips.

He finished his conversation and stood. "We meet again, Joss Miller. You've been quite busy." He walked around the desk and held out his hand.

I shook hands with him. His grip was firm and cool. I felt like he held my hand a little too long and pulled away with a quick tug and a smile. "I appreciate you taking the time to speak with me."

"Of course. I've been waiting to see if you would include me in your lineup for *Cold Justice* podcast. That's what we all want for Rebecca. Justice. Isn't that right, Miranda?"

Miranda stood by looking from Ethan back to me. She turned her body toward him and brushed a speck off his shoulder. "Of course. We miss her so much. I still can't believe someone took her life so senselessly."

While Miranda talked, Ethan gazed at me. His scrutiny made me want to squirm. Nervous, I started babbling. "I'm really looking forward to attending the gala next week. It will be my first time. I saw Synaptic is one of the major sponsors."

Ethan's face lit up with a smile. "I'm glad you'll be there, Joss. We're thrilled to be a part of the annual event. It's a great opportunity to showcase our latest AI advancements and connect with the art community. We have a lot of tools that might be of interest."

I nodded. "I actually use a Synaptic product to edit the audio for my podcast."

Ethan folded his arms. "Is that so? Miranda, we need to include Joss and the podcast in an ad. Do you have any sponsors yet, Joss?"

"Uhm, no. I'm not there yet."

He frowned. "No? You have to make some money off your hard work."

"Maybe, right now I enjoy producing the podcast."

He studied my face. I wasn't sure if that was disappointment on his face for my lack of business savvy or something else. I cleared my throat. "Is this still a good time?"

Ethan gave me a crooked, almost sheepish looking, smile. "Yes, of course. I'm sorry I keep staring at you. I know it's rude. From the first time I saw you at Magnolia Media, I thought there was something familiar about you. You remind me of Rebecca. Doesn't she, Miranda?"

Miranda turned to me, crossing her arms. "I kind of noticed that when I first saw you too. Not an exact match, but definitely the same complexion." She looked me up and down. "You're almost the same height, but she was smaller. Rebecca was a tiny thing."

Was that an insult?

I did my best to keep my face neutral. I had hips, but I didn't need someone else pointing that out.

Ethan asked, "So are you coming to the gala alone?"

Miranda looked at him, horror in her eyes. "Ethan, that's not an appropriate question?"

I didn't think so either. If Ethan had this flirtatious tone with most women, it would be hard to be in a relationship with him. I was no psychologist, but I detected a hint of narcissism. I wondered if this was how he had acted with Rebecca.

"I'll be there with my boyfriend." I replied, trying to keep my tone light but firm. If he followed social media, he already knew my man was a homicide detective.

But Ethan chuckled, seemingly unfazed by my response. "Of course, of course. A pretty woman like you would have a man. Miranda, you can leave us. I promise I will behave."

Miranda gave him a sharp look like she didn't quite believe him.

Ethan's expression hardened for a moment before he composed himself.

I didn't quite know what to think of this quiet exchange between them, but it made me even more uncomfortable.

Miranda turned toward me as if she wanted to say something. Instead, she walked out. I kind of hoped she'd stay. The silence felt deafening once the door closed behind Miranda.

"Please have a seat." Ethan beckoned me to a chair in front of his desk. He crossed back to the other side. With the long desk in between us, some of my discomfort lessened.

He sat down, his eyes still way too intense. "I apologize. It's been hard, losing her. I haven't been myself since they found…"

I nodded. "I understand. Losing someone you love is never easy. That's why I'm doing this podcast, to honor Rebecca's memory and maybe someone will come forward with information."

A LATTE MAYHEM

"We can only hope." Ethan pressed a key on his keyboard. The screensaver disappeared. "I appreciate you sending the questions ahead of time. That was thoughtful."

"I try not to pull surprises on my guests."

Ethan leaned forward. "Good. So, I can decline answering some of these questions?"

I hesitated. "Of course, which questions?"

He lifted his chin. "I won't talk about our relationship. I agree to tell you how we met but I've had too many people want to drag our relationship into tabloids and online gossip."

I pulled my phone out and placed it on his desk in front of me. "Okay, before I start recording, can I ask a question?"

He stared at me with that intense gaze of his. "Sure, I feel like I can trust you."

I took a breath, not sure if he would answer my question or kick me out of his office. "Some have speculated that you and Rebecca might have had a tumultuous relationship. What would you say to those who believe you had something to do with her death?"

Ethan looked at something behind me.

Curious, I glanced back. Outside the windows of his office, Miranda stood as if observing the interview. The door was closed shut, but I wondered if she could hear our conversation, like behind the one way mirror of an interrogation room.

I turned around to look at Ethan. "If you're not sure you want to do this interview, I can leave."

He lifted his hands from the desk as if in surrender. "No, I can do the interview. I just have a lot of nervous people around me. I am the face of Synaptic. I represent a lot of good people who work hard to deliver cutting edge products and I have an uptight board. I can't afford to mess up."

"I see." I wondered if Ethan had something to hide.

"You don't see." He smiled at me as if he had to explain to me like a little child. "I loved Rebecca. Like any couple, we had our ups and downs. We were both passionate people with strong opinions. We argued privately, sometimes publicly. But we always found a way to work through our issues. I would never have done anything to harm her."

He spread his hands on the desk as if to steady himself. "If she hadn't disappeared, I intended to propose to her. I already had the ring. But she was so deep into that canvas for the Ashford Art Gallery. It consumed her. It kind of felt like she let that be her only focus because she was running from something. And before you ask," he jabbed a finger toward me, "she wasn't running from me."

Before I could catch myself, I asked, "Are you sure? She told Olivia she intended to leave Charleston."

Ethan opened his mouth, confusion on his face. "What?"

He didn't know that? Was he playing a game?

He held up a finger. "Excuse me for a minute."

I started to say something, but shut my mouth. Red splotches had formed along his jawline. With a bit of horror, I rose from my seat as Ethan snatched open the door. He strode toward a bewildered Melinda.

Before the glass door shut, I heard him say, "Did you know—?"

The glass was pretty solid. All I could see was Ethan waving his arms around while Miranda stared at him. He must have said something untoward to her. Her pleasant face turned almost ugly as she snarled and hurled something back at him.

Whatever she said, Ethan stepped back like the steam had been let out of him.

Miranda stabbed an accusatory finger in his direction before stomping off, her hair flying in the wind of her exit.

I turned around quickly. I didn't want Ethan to know I saw what transpired. I mean how could I not miss the show? My only regret was I couldn't hear a thing they said to each other.

Eleanor told me there were rumors that Rebecca was leaving Magnolia Media. Why would Rebecca leave a PR company that had represented her all those years and a woman who was supposedly a friend? And how did a man who wanted to propose to a woman not know what she was going through?

I waited, almost holding my breath until Ethan returned. He straightened his tie and sat back in his desk chair. Other than the redness still prevalent around his face and a stray hair, he appeared composed. I watched him with bated breath.

His gaze landed on me, almost as if he'd just remembered I was still in his office. "Shall we begin?"

I nodded and pressed record on my iPhone before he changed his mind.

COLD JUSTICE PODCAST

Season 2, Episode 5: The Boyfriend
Published: July 1

Joss: Welcome to another episode of the *Cold Justice* Podcast. Today, we'll be diving into the Rebecca Montgomery case from a new and intimate perspective - that of her then boyfriend, Ethan Turner. Ethan is a well-known figure in the tech world. He's the founder and CEO of Synaptic, a cutting-edge artificial intelligence company.

In this candid conversation, Ethan will be sharing his memories of Rebecca and their life together. He'll also be addressing the speculation and rumors that swirled around their relationship in the wake of Rebecca's disappearance.

This is the *Cold Justice* Podcast. Let's get into it!

Joss: Ethan, thank you for joining me today.

Ethan: Thank you for having me, Joss. I'm glad to be here and thank you for your platform. You have a refreshingly unique podcast.

Joss: I appreciate it. It's so many true crime podcasts, I hoped I could stand out from the crowd.

Ethan: You're doing a great job.

Joss: (clears throat) Let's start with your relationship with Rebecca Montgomery. How did you two meet, and what drew you to her?

Ethan: Rebecca and I met briefly as students at SCAD.

Joss: SCAD. That's Savannah College of Art and Design?

Ethan: That's correct (chuckles). A lot of people assume because I'm a tech guy and that I must have gone to MIT or Georgia Tech. But I graduated with a B.F.A. in User Experience Design. I picked up some coding along the way as a teenager, but I leave that to others to do here at Synaptic. I'm invested in interfaces, making our products ready for the future.

Joss: You mainly focus on artificial intelligence, but you also support the arts. Being a SCAD alumni, I can see why.

Ethan: Art has always been important to me. My mother was a painter. Still is. I learned early on to appreciate colors and styles.

A LATTE MAYHEM

Joss: You have fascinating artwork here at Synaptic. And that stunning mural in your lobby, Rebecca painted that. Didn't she? Can you tell us about how that project came together?

Ethan: Absolutely. When we were designing the new Synaptic building, I knew I wanted to incorporate art that would inspire our employees and visitors. Rebecca immediately came to mind. I knew she was here in Charleston and that she'd painted a few murals around the city.

Rebecca's unique style and vision were the perfect fit. I commissioned her to create a mural that would capture the essence of our company - the fusion of creativity and technology. She spent weeks working on it, pouring her heart and soul into every detail. The result is breathtaking, and it's a daily reminder of her incredible talent.

Joss: I also understand that Synaptic is a major sponsor of the upcoming art gala. Can you tell us more about your involvement and why you feel it's important to support the arts?

Ethan: I believe that creativity and innovation are the driving forces behind progress, whether technology or any other field. When I heard about the gala, I knew I wanted Synaptic to be a part of it (chuckles). It also helps that Vivian Ashford, the owner of the Ashford Art Gallery, is my aunt. Her late husband was my mom's brother.

Joss: I met and interviewed Vivian on an earlier episode. She told me she met Rebecca through you. Rebecca's last mural at the art gallery, I feel like she really poured herself into it. What do you think?

Ethan: Absolutely. I had a vision for what she painted here, and Rebecca followed my thoughts and made the vision come to life. But when Vivian asked Rebecca to do what she wanted (silent pause), she did. Day and night. Pure focus.

Joss: In the time leading up to Rebecca's disappearance, did you notice any changes in her behavior or mood?

Ethan: (silence, deep breath) She seemed more distant and preoccupied, but I figured it was because she was pouring all her energy into the mural. I tried to talk to her about it, but she assured me everything was fine. Looking back, I wish I had pressed harder, maybe then I could have helped her.

Joss: Many people, including your Aunt Vivian, noticed that Rebecca seemed paranoid. Are you sure you don't remember someone hanging around, calling her, or anything else that might have caused her distress?

Ethan: (hesitates, then sighs) You're right. Whenever I think back on that time, Rebecca did seem jumpy and on edge (pauses, collects his thoughts). There was one incident that stands out in my mind. We were having dinner at a restaurant down-

A LATTE MAYHEM

town, and suddenly, Rebecca's demeanor changed. She became visibly agitated and started looking around the room as if she'd seen a ghost. Before I could ask what was wrong, she bolted out of the restaurant. I ran after her, and when I caught up to her, she was wild-eyed and shaking (voice becomes strained). I tried to get her to tell me what had happened, but all she said was that she thought she saw somebody she never wanted to see again. She wouldn't go into any details, no matter how much I pressed her.

(takes a deep breath) After that, she started spending more and more nights at the gallery, working on the mural. My aunt Vivian mentioned that she'd increased security measures and even hired a security guard to watch over the gallery at night (shakes his head). I should have realized then that something was seriously wrong. Olivia, Rebecca's sister, mentioned Becca had recently had a mental breakdown. I guess I just wanted to believe that everything would be okay.

Joss: One last question, Ethan. If Rebecca were here today, what would you want to say to her?

Ethan: (takes a deep breath) I would tell her how much I love her and miss her every single day. I'd tell her that I'm sorry I couldn't protect her, and that I won't rest until I find out what happened to her. Rebecca was the love of my life, and a part of her will always be with me.

Joss: Thank you, Ethan, for your honesty and for sharing your story with us.

Ethan: Thank you, Joss.

Joss: That's all for today's episode. If you have any information that could help with the investigation, please reach out to the hotline the police have set up.

Monday, July 1, 8:45 p.m.

In record-breaking time, I published the fifth episode hours after I finished editing. Same day delivery. Ethan Turner's interview racked up more downloads than Olivia's did within the first hour.

"Did I do the right thing?" I asked Andre in between taking bites of pizza. Andre wasn't a fan of pineapples, but I'd been craving a Hawaiian pizza. Like a caring boyfriend, he ordered a large pizza, half Hawaiian and half meat.

He grimaced. "People are curious about Rebecca's boyfriend, and up to this point, he's been quiet. Rarely has he given any interviews about her. From the outside, his focus appears to be all about his company. He opened up to you."

"I don't know what's going on, but I'm grateful. This season most of my guests wanted to set the record straight or they felt I was trustworthy enough to spill their guts."

Andre pulled one of my curls. "You are a good person and it radiates from you."

"When I mentioned Rebecca's plans to leave Charleston, it looked like he genuinely had no idea. In fact, he flew out of the room and said something to Miranda. But shouldn't he have known if they were as close as he claimed?"

Andre nodded, reaching for another slice. "Maybe Rebecca kept her plans from him for a reason."

"That could be true. When you and Beckett talked to people, did anyone mention if Ethan had a temper or anything?"

Andre shook his head. "No. He mainly gets glowing reviews about the products he makes. He's seen as a golden boy here in Charleston because he's bringing a taste of Silicon Valley to the city. I don't know, Ethan could be a decent guy, but I'm skeptical. A few people mentioned he was intense behind the scenes, especially about meeting product deadlines."

I shrugged. "That could be any boss or CEO. They want the product to succeed so they can rake in the profits. I sure wish I could have heard what he and Miranda argued about. I wonder if he thought Miranda knew but didn't tell him. The only person who admitted Rebecca's desire to leave Charleston was Olivia. Doesn't that seem strange too?"

Andre threw the crust on the plate. He tended to not eat the crust, whereas I loved bread. I devoured my entire pizza. Probably explained why Andre ate a lot more pieces than me. He reminded me of how my brother used to eat. Must be a guy thing.

"Most people who were close to Rebecca didn't seem to know her as well as they thought. I got the impression that she was an incredibly private person, which makes it much harder to investigate someone who was such a closed book."

My phone pinged next to me. When I glanced at my phone, I saw that Simone had finally responded. "Oh, I've been waiting on this email."

I clicked on my email and read it.

Subject: Re: Rebecca Montgomery - Cold Justice Podcast

Hey Joss,

It's so good to hear from you. I apologize for the delayed response to your email. Things have been quite hectic at the university lately. Yes, I have been listening to the Cold Justice Podcast. Loved your first season and have been keeping up with the current season too. I was tickled to see my sister's name in the credits for audio mixing. Good to hear you and Nyla are still keeping in touch after all these years.

I'm so saddened by the loss of Rebecca to the art world and ... well, the world in general. I do remember Rebecca from her time in Savannah. We weren't friends, but we spoke to each other during faculty and campus events. She was an incredibly talented artist with a unique perspective, and her students loved her.

While I don't have any specific information about her disappearance. I do recall some rumors. Let me first say I'm not comfortable with spreading gossip. I do know there were quite a few theories about why she left Savannah. Rebecca said her mother was ill and she wanted to return home. But I also heard it may have been something else.

I am more than happy to discuss with you in person. As it happens, I will be in Charleston for the gala at Ashford Art Gallery. I'm so honored this year that they will be featuring some of my photographs on display.

Please let me know if you would like to schedule a time to meet while I'm in town.

Looking forward to seeing you soon.

Best regards,

Simone

Excitement rose up in me. I didn't know why, but I felt like Simone might have the answers I'd been looking for. She touched on something that had been nagging at me about Rebecca's past.

"What's going on?" Andre asked.

I jumped a little at the sound of Andre's voice. I'd zoned out, deep in thought about what Simone may know.

"Um," I hesitated. I hadn't mentioned to Andre about digging into Rebecca's background at SCAD. "There is something I haven't told you. I'm not sure if it's relevant, but there could be an angle."

He eyed me. "So that email you were intensely reading has to do with Rebecca Montgomery. I thought you weren't investigating."

"I'm not." I protested a bit too loudly. I shut my eyes and blew out a breath. "Look, I reached out to a person I know who teaches at SCAD. Simone Masters. She's Nyla B's older sister. I was curious if she knew Rebecca. She's coming to town for the gala and offered to meet."

Andre rubbed his hands across his face. "So you're looking into, but technically not investigating, Rebecca's time in Savannah. Why didn't you tell me about this?"

I shrugged, feeling a twinge of guilt. "I wasn't sure if it would lead anywhere. But now that Simone's coming, I think it could be a good opportunity to learn more about Rebecca's time there."

Andre's gaze sharpened, his eyes scanning my face. "What do you hope to find out?"

"If Rebecca was running away from something or someone. I know logically she came back to help out with her mother, but you guys focused on Claude and Ethan. And frankly…"

I stopped as something occurred to me.

Andre reached for me. "What? Joss, what's up?"

I looked over at him. "You heard the recording. Ethan met Rebecca in Savannah. Wait, I need to get this timeline straight."

"Timeline?" Andre threw up his hands. "Okay, for someone not investigating a murder, you're throwing around a lot of terms that say otherwise."

"Okay, okay. I want to know what happened to her, like you and everyone else. The Savannah angle may be something to consider. Simone will be at the gala. There will be an exhibit of her photography so that may not be the best time to talk."

"Oh, woman." Andre leaned his head back on the couch as if he had a headache.

I reached over and took Andre's hand in mine. "Hey, I want to help in any way I can. If there's something in Rebecca's past that could shed light on what happened to her, don't you think it's worth looking into?"

Andre met my gaze and sighed. "You're right. I'm sorry for getting frustrated. It's … this case has been weighing on me. I want to find answers for Rebecca's family and friends."

"I know you do." I scooted closer and wrapped my arms around him in a comforting hug. "I know you want me to stay out of this. I'm not trying to hinder your investigation. I've got your back."

His mouth slowly widened into a grin before wrapping his strong arms around me and pulling me close against his chest. "I've never had a woman quite like you in my life, Joss Miller," he murmured into my hair.

I smiled and nuzzled into his embrace. The last thing I wanted was for Andre to be mad with me.

Chapter 15
Gala Fireworks

Saturday, July 6, 7:06 p.m.

The week flew by in anticipation of the upcoming gala. Leesa went with me to pick out a dress. After three formal dress boutiques and trying on countless dresses, despite being bone tired, I finally hit gold late Wednesday afternoon. Literally. I'd never before bought anything that shimmered like fourteen karat gold.

When I stepped out of the dressing room, Leesa exclaimed. "Ooh, it's perfect. Andre is going to love this on you. Look how it shimmers in the light."

I decided not to show Andre the dress until Saturday.

Since Fay was also attending the gala, she closed the café earlier than usual. The week had gone better, even though the broken window still needed to be replaced. Thankfully, the insurance funds had been deposited, leaving Fay with the task of finding a window installer. She still fretted about having to pull money together for the back camera. Joe thought she should add more cameras around the café, but Fay protested about appearing like Big Brother or Big Sister inside.

With less than two hours before the gala began, I applied my makeup and removed the bonnet from my hair, fluffing my curls. Then I twirled in front of the full length mirror to study my final look. The dress's V-neckline plunged enough to be elegant without being too revealing and the dress cinched at my waist. I loved the delicate gold leaf embroidery that shimmered subtly under the light.

I turned to the side. A similar V-neck design showed my backside. The leaves cascaded down the back of the skirt. I felt like a piece of art as I lifted my leg. The strappy, gold colored heels I'd found on a mad dash to the mall were a perfect complement to the dress. I couldn't even remember the last time I'd been to a mall. Over the past few years, I've ordered most of my clothing online.

The doorbell chimed throughout the house making Minnie and Mickey scatter from my bedroom. In their exit, white fur flew in the air.

"Andre is here." My grandmother called up.

"I'm coming." I had a moment of déjà vu remembering my high school prom. A decade ago, I'd gotten dressed up like this, but it was my dad who called upstairs. The dress I'd worn was quite different from this one, but I remembered feeling like a princess.

I took my time down the stairs. Andre was waiting for me at the bottom. The smile that stretched across his handsome face made me feel even more beautiful.

My grandmother stood off to the side with her hands clasped together. "Oh my goodness, Joss! You look like a princess. And Andre is your Prince Charming. What a gorgeous couple."

I blushed over my grandmother's words. But she was right. The tux Andre wore tonight was a different cut from the one he'd worn at the wedding a few weeks before. This one fit him even sharper. I hadn't seen him clean-shaven in weeks. It was nice to see his jawline as he grinned at me.

My foot hit the last step, and he held out his hand for mine. As I placed my hand in his, I felt that electrifying energy that often passed between us. Andre gazed into my eyes, and I felt like he could see me – inside out.

"I'm a very blessed man to have you on my arms tonight."

I blushed like a schoolgirl. "Thank you."

The ride downtown to the art gallery was filled with soft jazz. Thankful for the cool air on my skin, I relaxed as Andre glided through traffic.

Andre said, "I know tonight will have us running into people who knew or are curious about Rebecca Montgomery, but I do want us to enjoy the evening."

"I plan to. This outfit took a lot to pull together."

He chuckled. "You look beautiful, Joss."

Tonight the gallery appeared a bit different than when I visited a few Sundays ago for the tea. As I stepped into the grand ballroom, the gala's interior decorations took my breath away. The room was adorned with stunning artwork, and the soft glow of the chandeliers cast a warm light over the well-dressed attendees.

To my surprise, several people approached me throughout the evening expressing their admiration for my podcast and my dedication to uncovering the truth about Rebecca's disappearance. It was both flattering and unnerving to realize the episodes had garnered so much attention and that people knew who I was.

As I mingled with other guests, I caught sight of Ethan. And then Miranda. Apparently they had not made up yet after the argument I witnessed earlier this week. Or maybe they were keeping their relationship low-key. Either way, while Ethan greeted guests with a smile, Miranda seemed to be watching him. And her sister, the receptionist I'd met when I went to interview Miranda, stood next to her, keeping an eye on her older sister.

My guess was Miranda knew more about what was going on with Rebecca than she claimed. She had to have known Rebecca wanted to leave Magnolia Media. Probably because Miranda had her eyes on Ethan.

I looked around for Ethan's Aunt Vivian but didn't see her.

I did see Eleanor approaching me in a hurry. The author looked worried.

She walked up to us. "Hello, Detective Baez. Don't you look dabber tonight and, Joss, you look gorgeous in gold. It's so flattering against your skin tone."

"Thank you, Eleanor. You look beautiful as well." I frowned at her. I saw this woman almost every weekday at the café so I could tell when something was wrong. "Are you okay?"

Eleanor glanced at me and then Andre. "Have either of you heard?"

"Heard what?"

Her voice shook slightly. "They're trying to keep this low key. I don't know why. I guess because she's ... alive."

The alarm that I felt appeared on Andre's face. He touched Eleanor's arm. "Wait, what? Eleanor, start at the beginning."

I rubbed her other arm.

Eleanor gulped and took a deep breath. "Vivian was leaving the gallery late last night. She was walking to her car when a car came speeding out of nowhere. It jumped the curb. It didn't hit her, but it startled her enough to make her fall. She's a much older woman than she appears. I saw her earlier and she has a broken hip. She's going to be down for some time. Oh, she was so upset about missing tonight."

I exchanged looks with Andre. "What happened to the car?"

Eleanor shook her head, her eyes angry. "The car didn't stop. It sped off into the night, leaving her there, badly injured and alone. It's like they didn't even care whether she lived or died. Sorry, I'm shook up after seeing Vivian. She put so much energy into this event. And she's so vibrant." Eleanor took my hands. "Please enjoy yourself. I know it's your first time at the gala. But I thought you should know."

Eleanor waved at someone behind us and went to talk to them.

I hooked my arm inside of Andre's. "Do you think—"

He peered down at me. "Hey, I know that look on your face. Vivian will be alright. I'm sure someone will catch who did this."

I sighed. "I know. I can't help but think this wasn't a random accident. What if someone deliberately targeted Vivian? You know she was on my podcast."

Andre frowned. "She didn't say who the killer was, Joss."

"No, but what if she said something that spooked someone."

Andre's face grew thoughtful as if he was considering what I said. We didn't have time to talk about it. I looked up and Ethan was coming toward us.

"Joss, it's so good to see you. Lovely dress." He commented, looking me up and down.

Andre tensed beside me.

"Thank you."

Ethan held out his hand. "And you are Detective Baez. We haven't had the chance to meet, but I've become acquainted with your partner — Beckett."

For a moment, I wasn't sure if Andre was going to reciprocate, but he took the man's hand and shook it. "Good to meet you in person."

Ethan looked from me to Andre. "The detective and the podcaster, you are a good looking couple. Thanks for coming out to the gala tonight."

"How's your aunt? I'm sorry to hear about her injury. She was really great to talk to."

Ethan's smile faltered. He licked his lips. "She's doing as well as can be expected. She certainly has a lot of healing time ahead of her. Hopefully the cops will find out who's responsible for last night's hit and run. We wouldn't want another mystery to go too long without solving."

Miranda and her sister approached us.

"Hey, Miranda, Angie." I said.

Miranda smiled at me, but her smile didn't reach her eyes. She glanced at Ethan, but Ethan refused to acknowledge her. With a nod to me and Andre, he moved on to other guests.

Angie looked nervously from her sister to Ethan's backside. She commented. "I've been listening to your podcast. It's really good."

Miranda whipped back around toward us. "Yes, great job, Joss. And that's a lovely color. Did you know gold was one of Rebecca's favorite colors?"

"Uh, no, I didn't."

Miranda nodded. "Looks good on you. We should talk in the future about some PR for your podcast. It still stands too if you want Synaptic to be a sponsor. I'm sure Ethan would love that. Angie can set something up for you next week."

Angie looked at me as her sister walked off in the other direction. She shrugged. "Let me know and I can email you some meeting times."

I gulped, not looking at Andre. I knew he would have some words to say about that proposition. "Nice offer, but I may take a break from podcasting. It's a lot of hard work."

Angie smiled. "I'm sure it is. Enjoy your evening. I need to catch up with my sister."

As I knew he would, Andre questioned. "Sponsor?"

I waved my hand. "I mentioned that I'd been using Synaptic's editing software and they offered a sponsorship and some ad promotion."

Andre eyed me. "Doesn't sound like a good idea."

I started to retort back, but noticed a hush had fallen over the room. I turned toward the door to see who had caused the crowd to quiet. I frowned. "Claude?"

Claude had gone into his cave after the podcast. I'd reached out to him, but then I got busy interviewing people. I almost didn't recognize him tonight. He'd cut off his goatee and the man bun was gone. I'd never seen Claude with a haircut before.

Fay and Joe must have slipped in after us. They went over to Claude and started talking to him. I wasn't sure why the noise level quieted when he entered, but everyone returned to what they were doing.

Out of the corner of my eye, I saw Ethan. From across the ballroom, he'd locked eyes with Claude. It could have been my imagination but it was clear there was no love lost between the two men.

Why did Claude decide to come to the gala?

Saturday, July 6, 8:14 p.m.

Andre and I made our way over to Claude, Fay and Joe. Fay gushed, "Joss, look at you. You look gorgeous."

"Thank you." I glanced at Claude. "You too." Fay had her locs down tonight and wore a long black dress with a menagerie of tiny gold chains hanging at different lengths in the front. She looked stunning, like a model.

Joe beamed with pride next to her, dressed in black tux with a gold tie and cummerbund. They matched each other.

I turned to Claude. "This is a surprise. You cleaned up pretty nice."

He chuckled. "I figured it was time to stop hiding. Plus, I finished the canvas."

I sucked in a breath. "The one you were working on of Rebecca?"

"Yeah, I met with Vivian earlier this week and she loved it. It's going to be revealed tonight." Claude looked around. "Where is Vivian?"

I told the others about Vivian's hit-and-run accident.

Fay was the first to speak. "That is horrible for someone not to stop and help her. Could the driver have been drunk?"

Andre tilted his head. "It's possible. I will see what more I can find out about it from the report."

Claude remained silent for a moment, his expression troubled. When he finally spoke, his voice was heavy with emotion. "I can't believe someone would want to hurt Vivian. She's such a kind and generous person. She was emotional after seeing the painting of Rebecca."

"I saw it in its beginning stages. I can't wait to see the final version. Will it still be revealed tonight?"

Claude looked up at the stage. His eyes now hard. "We'll see. I guess it depends on what Ethan has to say about it since Vivian isn't here."

We all turned to find Ethan behind the podium, behind him was a covered canvas. He held up his hands to quiet the gala attendees. The room fell silent, anticipation heavy in the air.

Ethan began to speak, "Some of you may have heard that unfortunate circumstances has caused my aunt Vivian to be unable to attend the gala this evening. She worked hard on this event all year long. She has a long recovery ahead of her, but I promised I would unveil this special painting, a new piece from an artist who's never before been featured at the gallery."

Ethan looked off into the crowd. I felt like his eyes passed over me before landing on Claude.

"Claude McKnight, we welcome you to the Ashford Art Gallery. I haven't seen this yet, but I understand it's simply titled *Becca*."

I felt a wave of curiosity wash over me as Ethan gripped the sheet covering the canvas and, with a swift motion, pulled it down. I gasped along with others around me.

There, on the canvas, was a stunning depiction of Rebecca Montgomery. Her caramel skin seemed to glow, and her fiery copper dreadlocks were captured in vivid, lifelike detail. Claude had painted her with a paintbrush in her hand, as if she were in the midst of creating her own masterpiece.

Ethan, clearly choked up with emotion, stood and stared at the painting. He pulled a handkerchief out of his jacket and wiped his face. When he faced the crowd, his face was red. "Um, Aunt Viv gave me some notes. She wanted the painting to hang near the *Black Girl Magic* mural." He looked up, eyes shining. "Thank you, Claude, for capturing Rebecca's beauty and essence so perfectly."

I smiled as the two men exchanged looks. The animosity that existed between them earlier seemed to be replaced by a mutual respect.

Saturday, July 6, 9:34 p.m.

We'd finally made it to one of the most extravagant parts of the gala. The food. I added an assortment to my plate that included mini quiches with spinach and feta, bite-sized crab cakes, and skewers featuring ripe cherry tomatoes, creamy mozzarella, and fragrant basil leaves. Andre and Joe dived into the roast beef swimming in a succulent gravy. Fay and I both splurged with no shame over the chocolate fountain surrounded by fresh strawberries, pineapple chunks, and marshmallows for dipping.

While we ate, I looked around at the other guests attending the gala. Miranda stood talking with the mayor and a few other local politicians. She certainly made it her business to network.

I even saw Rick Nelson, who got an eye roll from Fay. Unfortunately, whoever threw the brick must have had sense enough to wear gloves. There were no fingerprints found.

I caught a glimpse of Liam Holbrook sneaking around the edges of the gala with a plate in his hands. I wondered how he'd managed to gain entry to such an exclusive event. He somehow got into Vivian's tea party the other weekend too. Thankfully, tonight had been pretty bland. No drama or outbursts for him to include on his social media tonight.

After we made our way through the other artists on display, Andre and I rounded the corner. He'd glimpsed the *Black Girl Magic* mural when we came in, but there were too many people standing in front of it. Now we could really look at it up close.

While Andre admired the infamous mural, I spotted familiar faces. "Nyla, Simone!" I called out, waving to get their attention.

Both Nyla B and Simone turned and made their way over to us.

Nyla hugged me. "Hey, girl. I was just telling Simone I knew you were here some place."

"Joss, so good to see you," Simone said, also giving me a warm hug. "And who's this handsome gentleman?"

I grinned, turning to introduce Andre. "This is Detective Andre Baez. Andre, you know Nyla. This is Simone Masters, her sister. I told you she knew Rebecca in Savannah."

Andre extended his hand, shaking Simone's firmly. "Pleasure to meet you, Simone. Joss has told me a lot about you."

Simone nodded, her expression turning serious. "Joss, I'm glad I caught you. I have to leave town in the morning, but there's something I think you should know about Rebecca's time in Savannah."

I felt my heartbeat quicken. "What is it, Simone?"

She glanced around, lowering her voice. "There was a rumor going around about a student who was stalking Rebecca. He'd been in her class. Rebecca was pretty friendly with her students. Apparently, this guy mistook her kindness for something else."

Andre leaned in, his brow furrowed. "Do you know who the student was?"

Simone shook her head. "No, I'm sorry. It was just a rumor I'd heard through the grapevine. But between that and her mother's illness, it's no wonder Rebecca decided to leave Savannah. She really did enjoy teaching, though. She was a favorite among the students."

A stalker student could definitely be a lead worth pursuing. "Thank you, Simone. This is really helpful information."

Simone smiled, squeezing my hand. "I hope it helps you find out what happened to her, Joss. Rebecca was a special person, and she deserves justice."

Simone and Nyla excused themselves to mingle with the other guests, and I turned to Andre, my eyes wide with excitement. "A stalker, Andre. That could be the missing piece you and Beckett have been looking for."

Andre nodded. "It's definitely worth looking into. I need to run it by Beckett and find out if we have any contacts at Savannah PD."

It could have been nothing. Once Rebecca left Savannah, she could have left it all behind her. Or did trouble follow her back home to Charleston?

Chapter 16
The Reckoning

Monday, July 8, 7:54 p.m.

All weekend, I couldn't shake the feeling that Vivian's hit and run accident was somehow connected to my podcast. The thought that my interview with her might have put her in danger made my stomach churn. I listened to her interview again several times and couldn't figure out if I was being paranoid.

Andre tried to convince me that it could have been a drunk driver or a tourist acting erratic.

As I swept the café floor, I thought back to the brief conversation with Simone. The student who had developed an unhealthy obsession with Rebecca had also been intriguing. What happened to that student after Rebecca left SCAD?

There were so many questions surrounding Rebecca and no answers in sight.

Fay, who had been counting the money from the register, paused and looked up at me with concern while I put away the broom and dustpan. "Honey, you have that thinking too hard face on. We've already had a hard, busy day. We need to wrap up this closing so we both can get out of here."

I sighed, reaching for trash bags. "I know. It was nonstop busy today with all the buses of people. Thank goodness for tourist season."

"Yeah." Fay threw her hands in the air. "I'm glad the boarded up window didn't drive people away. I had someone ask me if we were prepping for hurricane season."

I laughed, "Well, we are in the thick of it. Let's hope those storms stay off the coast. We've been pretty lucky the last few years."

Fay stomped her feet. "Amen to that!"

"Seriously, I can't shake the feeling that we're missing something. Rebecca's mental anguish — someone was responsible for what happened to her. I bet you that same someone warned me to stay away from this case."

"That was a troll trying to get under your skin and cause trouble. Besides, I'm sure Andre and his partner are on the case. You're finished with the season, right?"

I frowned. "I've interviewed all the people I wanted to. I didn't set myself up as an investigator. Still, I feel like I want to solve this, you know."

Fay glanced at the clock. "Well, I think you should take a break. Are you about finished out there? This is much easier when both of us are closing."

"Yeah, I'm almost ready to head out. It was a full weekend with the gala, and yesterday afternoon I stopped by my aunts. This time my mom and my grandmother came too."

Fay flashed a surprised look. "How did that go? How is your mom adjusting to her biological mom?"

"It's getting better. Let me take out this trash and then we can lock up."

I cringed as I shoved the back door. It slowly creaked open after I put my weight on it. The door liked to get stuck in the summer due to the humidity. There was a streetlamp right above the dumpster, but it didn't do much to illuminate the pathway. When the empty Crafty Corner shop was open, the streetlamp in the back of that building brightened the fence between the café and the shop.

"Let's make this quick, Joss." I muttered to myself. Not only was it dark, it smelled awful. The dumpster pickup wasn't until Tuesday, so it was pretty full. I heaved open the door and slammed the two trash bags inside as quickly as I could. And then moved just as fast back to the back door. It always felt creepy back here. But tonight, I felt especially on edge. And the sticky weather added to my misery.

Back inside, I secured the door, welcoming the cool air again.

Fay stepped out of her office with her bag on her shoulder. "All set?"

"Yes. Just need to wash my hands." The soapy water felt good after my jaunt out back to the dumpster. I removed my apron, stuffed it in the locker and grabbed my bag. Fay switched the lights off as we headed closer to the entrance.

While Fay locked up, I asked. "When do you think the window will be replaced?"

Fay sighed. "I have a few estimates that Joe helped me get. Hopefully, in another week or so. Joe's trying to get me to get this shatterproof glass with the insurance money, but then I would have to replace all the windows. And I don't have that kind of money."

We walked across the street to the parking lot together. "Maybe we can do the Friday Night Jams on more than one Friday. Those bring in a good bit of money."

Fay looked at me. "That sounds like a good idea, but it would be a lot of work."

A LATTE MAYHEM

I shrugged. "I can handle it."

Fay grinned. "Okay, well, let's talk about it tomorrow. Right now I'm too tired and I'm ready to put my feet up."

Once inside my car, I fumbled around with my phone. I noticed Andre had called. Before I checked the message, Fay honked her horn at me. I waved and watched her drive off. I decided I would listen to Andre's message when I got home and turned the key in the ignition.

But nothing happened.

I tried again.

"Oh no." Did the battery die? I slapped the steering wheel. There was always something wrong with this car. I pulled out my phone and called Andre, hoping he was off for the day.

"Joss, finally, I've been trying to get in touch with you."

"Oh, sorry. I'm just leaving work, but I have a problem."

"What's going on?" Andre's voice sounded tight.

"My car won't start. I think my battery died. Can you come pick me up?"

Andre blew out a breath. "Yes. I'm about a good fifteen minutes from you. Can you go back inside the café? Is Fay still there?"

"She already left. I'll text her and let her know I had to go back inside to wait for you."

"Alright. And, Joss, make sure you lock up behind you. I will be there soon."

It could have been my imagination, but Andre sounded worried. Or maybe it was me being paranoid. Again.

I sent a quick text to Fay, letting her know I needed to wait for Andre. I crossed the street, which was pretty quiet. After a struggle with the key, the café door opened. I closed and locked the door, the chimes loud in my ear.

I thought about sitting in a booth to wait for Andre, but that felt too vulnerable, so I went behind the counter toward the back. Sitting in Fay's office felt like a more secure plan.

I heard a noise before I rounded the corner and stopped. I grabbed the counter and stood still for what felt like a very long minute. When I didn't hear any more noise, I moved forward, peeking around the corner. Fay kept a light on above the sink across from the office. I stepped forward intending to head toward the office.

That's when I noticed.

The back door was open, just a crack.

I felt a chill run down my spine. I was sure I had closed and locked it earlier when I took out the trash. Was that the noise I'd heard?

I hesitated, a sense of unease washing over me. I had felt unsettled earlier when I was out back, but I couldn't quite put my finger on why.

Against my better judgment, I creeped toward the door, my heart pounding in my chest. Then I heard a noise behind me. Whirling around, I felt a scream catch in my throat. A figure loomed in the shadows, their features obscured by the darkness.

The figure stood between the back door and the way back up front.

What I knew for sure, I wasn't going out the back door.

Instinctively, I grabbed the nearest object I could find. Next to me was the cart that held the heavy baking pans Fay used. She had them ready to go for when she arrived in the morning.

A man's voice spoke from the dark corner of the room. "I told you to leave it alone, but you didn't listen."

The voice was raspy, but familiar. "Who are you?"

Something snapped in his hand like a rope. Then he was running toward me, his feet pounding against the tiled floor. I grabbed the cart with the pans and swung it around. My attacker crashed into the cart. Pans went flying everywhere. I grabbed one and held it out in front of me like a shield.

I had no idea how far away Andre was, but I needed to fight.

Expletives flung from the man as he shoved the cart out of his way.

I swung the large metal pan and felt the satisfying thud of metal against flesh. When he went down, I spun toward the front of the café.

Strong hands gripped my ankle and I screamed, bringing the pan down on his head again. Then the light over the sink showed my attacker's face.

And the hatred in his eyes.

How did I miss this?

Monday, July 8, 8:23 p.m.

"You?" I whispered. I backed up as I stared into the eyes of the last person I ever expected to see. I should have been running, but shock had me frozen in place.

Liam smiled, a cold, cruel twist to his lips. "Surprised to see me, Joss? You're better than I thought for a barista. You're getting too close to the truth, and I can't let that happen."

A LATTE MAYHEM

He advanced on me, his eyes glinting with malice. "You know, Joss, you and Rebecca aren't so different. Both friendly do-gooders."

I felt my back hit the wall, and I realized I was trapped. "What did you do to Rebecca?" I demanded, my body shaking.

He chuckled, a low, menacing sound. "What I had to do. What I'm going to do to you."

He lunged at me again.

But this barista knew her way around the café. This was my second home.

I ducked and spun around the corner. I grabbed the heavy metal carafe which I wished was filled with hot, steaming coffee. It packed a punch when I hit Liam square in the face. Blood spurted from his nose and he howled. "You—"

He grabbed his nose and glared at me. "You will die tonight, barista girl."

"Get down, Joss."

I knew the voice and I didn't hesitate. I slid to the floor as I heard a gunshot.

Liam roared before he swung around to flee out the back.

Next thing I knew, Andre was behind the counter beside me, his gun in his hand by his side. My knight in shining armor.

"Joss, are you alright?" His voice was tight with concern.

"Yes. He's getting away, Andre." I shouted.

"No, he's not." A voice yelled from the back.

Andre helped me up from the cold tiled floor, pushing me behind him as he advanced forward. I followed.

Andre's partner must have come through the back door. Beckett had Liam face down on the tile floor handcuffing him. Beckett grinned at me. "Looks like you had quite the fight in here, young lady."

I took a deep breath. "I know my way around this café. He got a pan to the head and a carafe to the nose."

Andre grabbed me in a one-arm hug. "Let's get you away from him."

Back in front of the café, blue lights lit up the street. I sighed. "I'm going to have to let Fay know what happened. At this rate, she might not want me around. The kitchen is a hot mess back there."

Andre guided me to a seat at the back of the café. "Sit. You're going to have to answer some questions. I will be right back."

I texted Fay, who promptly responded.

Fay: Oh no, Joss! I'll be right there!

From the safety of the booth, I watched two deputies lead Liam to a squad car. There was some satisfaction seeing the blood on his face.

Andre returned and sat across from me. "Didn't you get my message earlier?"

"What? Oh?" I rubbed my hands against my face. "I was planning to listen to it when I got home, but then the car wouldn't start. Why?"

Andre leaned back. "Well, as you probably figured out, Liam isn't who he says he is. I've spent the day looking into the information Simone told us."

I sucked in a breath. "Was he the student that harassed Rebecca? Wait, he said he went to the College of Charleston."

Andre held up a finger. "There was a Liam Holbrook who went to the College of Charleston, but that guy..." Andre reached for my hand, "is not Liam Holbrook."

I was speechless.

Massaging the back of my hand, Andre asked. "Are you okay? Should we take you to the hospital?"

"No. I mean I'm shocked, but not in shock. Once Fay gets here, and after I give my statement I just want to go home and take a shower. Then, you need to tell me everything."

Monday, July 8, 10:05 p.m.

Andre insisted on taking me back to his place. I rarely did overnights with him, but I was more shaken up by the ordeal than I thought. While I let the steamy water from the shower hit my back, the adrenaline left my body. Through tears, I thanked the Lord for my life and the timing of Andre and Beckett's arrival. A few minutes later, and I wasn't sure if my heroics would've saved me at all.

I'd called my grandmother to let her know what happened.

My grandmother comforted me. "It's good that you're with Andre. Let him take care of you. I will see you in the morning."

She didn't have to tell me twice. Wrapped in a warm blanket and nursing a cup of hot tea, I settled onto Andre's couch.

He sat down beside me. "You can sleep in the bed and I can take the couch."

"No, no. You have a comfortable couch. I will be fine. Thanks for letting me crash here for the night."

He smiled and rubbed my shoulders. "Of course. Did you want something to eat? I know it's late, but you haven't eaten."

I shook my head. "My stomach feels queasy. The hot tea is fine."

Andre reached for my chin and turned my face toward him. "Look, I know you have a lot of questions, but you've been through an ordeal. You should get some sleep."

"I will sleep better once I know who Liam really is and why he came after me." My voice broke and I could feel a tremble travel down my arm to my hand.

Andre grabbed the cup of tea and set it on the coffee table. He pulled me closer to him. The warmth of his body plus the blanket soothed my nerves.

Andre took a deep breath. "The man we've been calling Liam Holbrook is actually Caleb Davenport."

I felt a chill run down my spine. "What happened to the real Liam? What's his connection to Rebecca?"

Andre's grip tightened around me. "First, Caleb was the student who stalked Rebecca in Savannah. At some point, she did get a restraining order against him. She decided to come back to Charleston to care for her mother and put the whole ordeal behind her."

"As far as Liam Holbrook... He was a real student from the College of Charleston. The actual Liam doesn't have much of a social media presence. From what we can ascertain, Caleb stole Liam's identity or at least borrowed the name. He started his

Shady Affairs social media accounts three years ago. We have a feeling he has other accounts too."

"Like that watcher account that sent me that weird message."

Andre nodded. "Probably so. We'll do a search of his place and get all his electronics once we have a warrant. I think we're going to be able to find a lot of information, even discover what might have happened to Rebecca."

The pieces of the puzzle were finally falling into place. "So, when Rebecca started gaining fame for her murals around Charleston, especially that one at Synaptic, Caleb must have discovered her location. He was probably the one bothering her while she worked on the *Black Girl Magic* mural."

Andre blew out a breath. "I think you're right, Joss. And with your podcast gaining traction, he must have seen an opportunity to insert himself into the narrative, to try and control the story."

I shuddered, remembering all the times I had interacted with Liam. Caleb. "He was hiding in plain sight. I mean the guy was earning money by doing what people love the most – checking out gossip."

Andre pulled me closer, his arms wrapped around me in a comforting embrace. "He fooled everyone, including the police. But now that we know the truth, we can make sure he pays for what he's done."

I leaned against Andre. "Mr. Shady Affairs is going to get a taste of his own medicine. I hope I broke his nose."

Andre chuckled, and then I started giggling.

It was no laughing matter, but I was grateful I'd survived the ordeal.

I couldn't imagine what Rebecca had gone through with that psycho.

Epilogue

Three Months Later

Friday Night Jam
September 13, 6:30 p.m.

 Fay wanted me to take some time away from the café after my ordeal. But for the rest of the summer, I continued like normal. Or as normal as I could. Fay and I closed together and she made sure I left the parking lot first.

 The window and the back camera were both replaced. Fay even had floodlights installed over the door that illuminated the dreaded path to the dumpster.

 What really brought me joy.

 Fay compromised and let me coordinate the Friday Night Jam twice a month. We got enthusiastic responses from the music community for the extra night. DJ Nyla B scheduled the Fridays on her calendar.

 I was grateful for all the support and well-wishers.

Without any prodding from anyone, I started back seeing a therapist. I hadn't reached out to one since Daddy died. I decided to try the online route, and it took a couple of tries before I found the right person to talk to. It was good to talk to someone, so I wouldn't worry my loved ones with my concerns.

My nightmares.

Some of the Shady Affairs trolls lingered, but it didn't take long to block most of them. The account magically disappeared. I doubt Liam/Caleb did it himself. Probably the higher ups wanted to scrub their social media platform of an influencer who spent time committing or attempting to commit murder.

As I approached the stage, I smiled, happy to see Andre and Joe setting up the equipment. Crime didn't stop in Charleston, but Andre found a way to be there for me. I spent a lot of time at his place. While it was nice, the arrangement was testing our celibacy vows.

Andre looked up and smiled when he saw me, his eyes sparkling with warmth. And concern. He was always worried about me.

"Hey, beautiful," he called out, hopping down from the stage to give me a quick kiss. "Ready for tonight?"

I nodded, feeling my cheeks grow warm at Andre's public affection. "It's a great lineup tonight."

Andre's expression turned serious for a moment and he took me to the side. "I wanted to let you know the trial date for Caleb has been set. With all the evidence we've gathered, I'm confident he'll be convicted."

I shuddered at the mention of Caleb's name. It had been three months since his arrest, and he had been behind bars without bail ever since. The thought of facing him in court was daunting, but I knew it was a necessary step in getting justice for Rebecca.

And for me. The man had traumatized me.

Fay rushed toward us. "Guys, did you hear the news? Rick Nelson's development plan was shot down again at the city council meeting, and this time it's for good!"

My eyes widened in surprise. "What? How?"

Fay grinned. "Vivian Ashford and Ethan Turner proposed the building next door be turned into the Rebecca Montgomery Art Center for children. Those two have a lot of clout and it was a unanimous vote. They must have made Rick a good deal; he didn't even balk about it."

Tears pricked the corners of my eyes. "That's incredible. So the café and other shops are safe?"

Fay nodded, her own eyes glistening. "There's more. Vivian wants to meet to discuss how to include the café in the project. She wondered if we wouldn't mind opening up the wall and connecting the two spaces."

I gasped, clasping my hands together. "Fay, that's awesome."

"Yes," she nodded. "That space would also give us more room for these Friday Night Jams. We are stretching the capacity of this space back here."

I couldn't help but shout, "God is good!"

Fay threw up her hands. "All the time!"

We finished setting up and opened the doors for the waiting crowd. It was all hands on deck for every barista tonight as we filled orders.

After about an hour, Fay came up to me. "Girl, take a break. You're working too hard, making the rest of us look bad." She winked at me. "Go hang out with your man. You don't want to leave him alone too long. Some other lady might get some ideas."

I grinned. "Thanks, Fay."

Andre saw me coming and pulled out a chair. I sat, grateful to be off my feet. I glanced over at him. "Hey, I noticed the date earlier when I was looking at my phone. Can you believe it's been a year since we first met?"

"Really?" He hung his arm casually around the back of my chair. "Time flies when you're solving mysteries and chasing down bad guys."

I laughed. "Do you think the podcast has been more trouble than it's worth?"

Andre shook his head. "You're good at it. Just promise me you'll keep me in the loop in case I need to save you again." He grabbed my hand. "I have plans for you and me."

I tilted my head. "Do you? Are you going to share the details?"

He looked into my eyes while still holding my hand. "When the timing is right, absolutely."

Despite the crowd around us and the singer belting out a song from the stage, I was only aware of the man across from me.

Like I'd told my mother a few months ago.

I truly believed he was the one for me.

About the Author

Tyora Moody is the author of **Soul-Searching Mysteries,** which includes **cozy mystery, women sleuth mystery,** and **romantic suspense** under the Christian Fiction genre. Her books include the Eugeena Patterson Mysteries, Joss Miller Mysteries, Serena Manchester Mysteries, Reed Family Mysteries, and the Victory Gospel Mysteries.

When Tyora isn't working for a literary client, she's either loving on her cats, listening to an audiobook or podcast, binge-watching crime shows or Marvel movies, and of course, thinking about the next book.

To contact Tyora about reviewing her books or book club discussions, visit her online at TyoraMoody.com.

Join her newsletter at https://tyoramoody.substack.com/

Tyora Moody's Books

Eugeena Patterson Mysteries

Deep Fried Trouble, #1

Oven Baked Secrets, #2

Lemon Filled Disaster, #3

A Simmering Dilemma, #4

An Unsavory Mess, #5

A Spicy Predicament, #6

Marinated Conditions, #7

Eugeena Patterson Family Shorts

Shattered Dreams, #1

A Blended Family Christmas, #2

Falling in Love... Again!, #3

TYORA MOODY

Joss Miller Mysteries
Double Mocha Blues, #1
A Latte Mayhem, #2
Mint-Flavored Trouble, #3

Serena Manchester Mysteries
Hostile Eyewitness, prequel
Bittersweet Motives, #1
Dangerous Confessions, #2
Waning Innocence, #3
Presumed Guilty, #4
Shifting Blame, #5

Lowcountry Secrets (Romantic Suspense)
The Homecoming, #1

Reed Family Mysteries
Broken Heart, #1
Troubled Heart, #2
Relentless Heart, #3
With All My Heart, #3.5
Faithful Heart, #4
Wounded Heart, #5

Victory Gospel Series (Mysteries)
When Rain Falls, #1
When Memories Fade, #2
When Perfection Fails, #3

Victory Gospel Shorts (Sweet Romance)
The Replacement Date, #1
Southern Delights, #2
When Love Finds Me, #3
Nobody's Replacement, #4
A Southern Delights Christmas, #5
Holding on to Love, #6

Made in the USA
Middletown, DE
02 August 2024